Herbert E. Church, Richard Church, Alfred John Church

Making a start in Canada

Letters from two young emigrants

Herbert E. Church, Richard Church, Alfred John Church

Making a start in Canada
Letters from two young emigrants

ISBN/EAN: 9783742865014

Manufactured in Europe, USA, Canada, Australia, Japa

Cover: Foto ©Raphael Reischuk / pixelio.de

Manufactured and distributed by brebook publishing software
(www.brebook.com)

Herbert E. Church, Richard Church, Alfred John Church

Making a start in Canada

MAKING A START
IN CANADA

LETTERS FROM TWO YOUNG EMIGRANTS

WITH AN INTRODUCTION

BY

ALFRED J. CHURCH, M.A.

Professor of Latin in University College, London

LONDON

SEELEY & CO., ESSEX STREET, STRAND

1889

INTRODUCTION.

MANY young men of what is commonly called the upper middle class yearly leave their country to seek fortune, or, to put the case more modestly, subsistence, in Canada. It has occurred to me, having recently sent two sons to that country, to publish some extracts from the letters in which they have described their experience, and to say something about their preparations for this undertaking. Many parents will be glad, I imagine, to know how their sons should be equipped, and what is the sort of life which they actually lead.

My two sons, then, when they left England

for Canada, were aged respectively eighteen years one month and sixteen years nine months, and were both strong and well-grown. I mention this because many lads at the age of the younger of the two are quite unfit for the work which, as will be seen, fell upon them. This lad was nearly as tall as his brother (five feet eleven inches), and almost his match in strength. As the two were very closely attached to each other, and I looked for much advantage to both from their continued companionship, I did not like to separate them. Otherwise I should say that it would not be well to send out so young a lad.

They had been educated in the ordinary way at a Grammar School, and, for a short time before their departure, at University College, London. I can hardly say that any attempt had been made to specialize their education. Indeed, the idea of emigrating, though long cherished by them, did not take any definite shape till but a few weeks before it was carried into execution. If it had, I am not sure whether I should have cared to divert their attention from their general instruction. Still, I do not doubt that if they had realized the probability of their going to a country where both the French and German languages are spoken, they might have applied themselves with more diligence to these studies. When it had been determined that they should go, they attended, at the college, a course of lectures on practical geology. I very much regret that their teaching in this most valuable and interesting subject extended over so brief a time.

Of matters that were likely to be practically useful they learnt at home some simple operations in cooking ; for instance, how to make a suet pudding, to boil potatoes, and to make bread. They received instruction from a shoemaker, and under his supervision heeled, soled, and patched boots. They also learnt how to mend a rent in a coat and to darn a hole in a stocking. I am told, and I can well believe, that they lost much by missing what they might easily have got, and what is indeed within the reach of most lads: some practical instruction in farriery. There was a forge close to their home, where they might have learnt how to shoe horses, and acquired some elementary knowledge of the ordinary diseases of the animal, and of the remedies with which they are treated. If more time had been available, they might have attended classes at the Veterinary College. I am given to understand that even a very moderate skill in the veterinary art will be found one of the most profitable attainments that a lad can acquire.

They had the advantage of using a workshop belonging to a kind friend and neighbour. Here they had acquired some skill in carpentering, enough to enable them in a rude kind of way to set up, and even to construct, their own beehives. When it was settled that they were to go, they received some practical instruction from a skilled carpenter. They helped him to fence a field and to construct a wooden cow-house ; and they worked under his supervision for some days at various miscellaneous jobs.

The lads had, for several years before their departure, lived in the country, if one of the remoter suburbs of London can be called country. Here they had learnt something about gardening, and especially about the pruning of fruit-trees. They had kept pigs, which they managed themselves ; and they had also, in a small way, been bee-masters.

When the plan of emigration was matured, they attended the first course of lectures given by the Ambulance Association, having for its subject ' First Aid in Cases of Accident.' It is impossible to exaggerate the importance of this point. I should strongly advise all parents to insist upon their sons acquiring some elementary knowledge of what should be done in an emergency before the arrival of professional aid, often long delayed, as one may easily imagine, in a thinly-populated country. I say 'insist,' because they will probably find them unwilling or contemptuous, as my sons certainly were. Young people seem to count upon an immunity from accident, a delusion which their elders should not suffer to prevent them from acquiring the knowledge necessary for dealing with it in its first and most urgent needs. There is no necessity for pointing out how often health or life may be saved by presence of mind, guided by ever so little acquaintance with elementary medical facts. When I add that the lads had received some lessons in riding (they had not had, it will have been seen, that thorough country breeding of which riding is a necessary part), but that they were not so expert as they might advantageously have been, I have said enough on this part of my subject.

They took with them fishing-rods and tackle. I should particularly recommend, under this head, a good stock of artificial bait. In choosing a rod, particular care should be taken that the wood should be suitable to the climate, with its extremes of heat and cold, and especially its dryness. The tackle should not be too fine. They had also each a gun —it was a twelve-bore sporting-gun, one barrel choke, the other cylinder. They had a box of games, and a small chest with various medical appliances of the most necessary kind.

The list of the outfit which the two lads took with them is as follows (it must be remembered that they started their life in a gentleman's house, and therefore wanted some things which might not in every case be required) :

Dress suit.
Best tweed suit.
Tennis suit.
One cloth suit of 'leather suiting.'
Extra trousers of ditto.
The three suits that they had in wear.
Two pairs of corduroy trousers.
Ulster coat.
Pea jacket.
Mackintosh.
Dressing-gown (useful as an extra warm garment).
Twelve flannel shirts.
Two white shirts.
Four pyjamas (of flannel).
Four pairs winter and summer drawers.
Four vests.
Twenty-four pairs of socks.
Six collars (the flannel shirts being furnished with collars).

White cravats and cuffs.

Cardigan.

Two jerseys.

Twelve pocket-handkerchiefs (some coarse coloured handkerchiefs might be obtained in Canada).

Six Turkish towels.

Waterproof sheet (should be large, and of the best quality).

Blankets (should be an undivided pair of large size, and thick).

Rug.

Six pairs of dress gloves.

Three hedging and ditching ditto.

Two pair Canada mittens.

A housewife, with buttons, needles, etc., of all kinds (saddlery needles included).

One pair of high boots (others can be bought in Canada).

Pair of boots.

Dress shoes.

Pair of shoes (not nailed).

Pair of slippers.

Ambulance braces.

Helmet of Jäger wool.

Cholera belt.

Trunk (which should be of a manageable size).

[An indiarubber bath should have been added, and some coarse cotton shirts.]

Portmanteau for cabin.

I must express my hearty thanks to Mr. A. G. Bradley (22, Great George Street, Westminster), by whose means my sons were settled in their first home.

I think that I may mention the names of the two tradesmen who supplied the outfit in a manner that has given satisfaction both here and in Canada : they have gained considerable experience in finding out what is really suitable for the needs of young men thus emigrating :

Mr. C. T. Merryweather, tailor and outfitter, Bridgegate, East Retford.

Mr. F. T. Clark, bootmaker (same address).

It should be especially remembered that *pieces* for repair of garments should be sent out; also all old clothes available should be included. And let everything be made large. I may say that the total cost of outfit, voyage, and maintenance of the two lads for the first year, also of taking up and stocking land, has been less than £500. It may be done for a much smaller sum.

A. J. C.

CONTENTS.

PART I.

ONTARIO.

CHAPTER I.

CHAPTER II.

CHAPTER III.

CHAPTER IV.

CHAPTER V.

CHAPTER VI.

PART II.

EXPLORING BRITISH COLUMBIA.

CHAPTER VII.

CHAPTER VIII.

CHAPTER IX.

PART III.

ALBERTA.

CHAPTER X.

CHAPTER XI.

CHAPTER XII.

CHAPTER XIII.

CHAPTER XIV.

CHAPTER XV.

Making a Start in Canada.

PART I.

ONTARIO.

CHAPTER I.

Our New Home.—The First Week's Work.—A few
Birds.

June, 1886.—On Saturday we left Toronto
by the mid-day train, arriving here a few
minutes before six. The country through which
we passed was quite different to that between
Montreal and Quebec. There were still large
forests, but the fields looked more cultivated,
and we saw lots of large orchards. We saw
Lake Sincoe, and in the distance Barrie. This
is a splendid place, with a sort of rambling
old farmhouse, a large garden and orchard,
and lots of vines. The fruit has all done
blossoming and is forming fast. The farm is
chiefly arable ; there are only about fifty head

of cattle and a few horses. The birds here
are rather peculiar. A robin is about as big
as a thrush; blackbirds and canaries are flying
about in plenty. There are also plenty of
mosquitoes; but I have only been bitten
once, and that hardly itched at all. I en-
close a mosquito. Mr. and Mrs. B—— are
very nice people indeed. The family consists
of two sons and three daughters. We could
not get our big trunk—which the porters at
Euston christened the Woolwich Infant—
into the house for some time. At last one
of the doors was taken down, and then we
managed it.

We began work on Monday at six. This
work was loading manure from the barn-yard
into waggons, which were then drawn out to
the fields, a waggon being always waiting to
be filled. This was continued till eight,
when we went in to breakfast; breakfast consisted of fresh meat, tea, bread-and-butter,
and fruit. After breakfast we went to the

potato-pits to cut up potatoes for seed—the potatoes had to be cut into pieces containing one or two 'eyes;' the juice stains the hands very much, and we found it almost impossible to wash it off during the day, soap only making it worse. This work was kept on till twelve, when we returned to the house for dinner, consisting of roast mutton, potatoes, beans, and pudding. After dinner we planted potatoes till six; we had to plant each seed-potato by itself along a furrow; and being kept in a stooping posture the whole time our backs soon began to ache. At six we had a tea of bread-and-butter, stewed fruit, and tea; after tea we went into the garden and worked at getting the tennis-lawn into order. When it became dark we went into the house and played whist till ten o'clock, when we had a supper of bread-and-butter and milk, and then went to bed. The next morning, after the usual 'Tumble up, boys,' at our door, we started on the same work, and, indeed, kept it up just the same every day till Friday, all the potatoes being then sown.

On Friday morning we followed a plough on some quite new ground, our portion of the work being to make the sods stop in the places into which the plough turned them ; this had to be done with our hands, and as the sods were frequently of considerable length and size and very stiff, it was no easy job, and very exasperating when, after a frantic struggle to push a sod three or four feet long out of the furrow, you saw it slowly roll back into its former position. We had also to help the man at the plough to clear it of roots, of which there were plenty ; altogether one had to be pretty lively to keep up with the plough. We left off at eight to go to break-fast ; after breakfast we did odd jobs, such as helping to harness the horses and to fix up fences. After dinner we dug weeds in the fields, till tea at six ; after tea we went along the stream and shot a few birds, and came in at dark to play whist.

On Saturday we got up at six and fetched the cows in, and then watched them being milked till eight, when we had breakfast. After breakfast we worked in the garden, digging and spreading manure till twelve. After dinner we went along the creek with our guns and shot some chipmunks, a woodpecker and bee-bird, getting back about half-past four.

About ten that night there was an alarm that the colts had got on to the railway track ; we went out with one of the men to try and find them, but could not do so. As we then heard that there would be no more trains till Monday morning, we did not trouble any further. About half an hour later the boss came home, and we helped to put away his horses and 'rig.'

June.—Herbert and I went out shooting in

the bush the other day. He shot an eyeholder, a bee-bird, and a chipmunk ; and I
shot two chipmunks. An eyeholder is a bird
with a large beak like a woodpecker, a
red mark on its head and a black one on its
breast. Its wings underneath are a bright
orange. It is a splendid-looking bird. When
it is properly cured we will send the skin to
you. The eye-bird is small, with a black back,
white breast, and a crest of orange-red.
Chipmunks are little brown squirrels, with
dark stripes on their backs. Yesterday we
were sent out to chop down weeds some
distance off. We bird-nested at the same
time ; but we only found some young swal-
lows in the hole of a tree. There is a large
kingfisher here which we have tried to shoot,
but we have not succeeded yet, as it never settles.
We manage now to make our cartridges fairly
well. The tennis-court has now been marked
out, and we are going to challenge the B——
Club near here as soon as we have had some

practice. The mosquitoes have become perfectly awful. They make for my hands when I am asleep. They do not touch my face, but sometimes they bite my neck. I have about thirty bites on each hand, and as many on each of my feet. Socks are no protection at all; they manage to get through even the thickest. We get up about six o'clock, and bathe in the mill-pond, which is about twelve feet deep in the middle. On Sundays we have not much to do, and come down about eight. Altogether it is a very jolly life, though the work is hard. We have, however, plenty to eat, and as much time to ourselves as we want. There are plenty of places round about with any quantity of fish; but I have not tried yet, as the fish in the stream are only very small.

CHAPTER II.

June.—We had a tremendous thunderstorm here a few days ago. The rain came down in great sheets, and in a few minutes the road was turned into a stream six or eight inches deep. We managed to get into shelter just before it came on. On Friday afternoon we went to a garden-party nine miles off. There were six of us in a 'democrat,' a four-wheeled vehicle with two seats, one behind the other. The roads were very bad, and one or two hills were so steep that we had to walk up, and going down had to hold on to keep the 'rig' from overrunning the horses. It took three hours to do nine miles. We got home again about half-past nine. A lawn-tennis match was to have been played against a neighbouring club, but the rain prevented it. The strawberries have been on for some time now. The other day Mr. B—— took a hundred quarts to market. I am now learning to milk. At first I took half an hour to half-milk a single cow. Every morning Dick goes to bring the cows in, while I have to water and groom the driving-horse, and sometimes one or two colts, if they have been used, and to clean out their stalls before breakfast.

This morning when I took Tiny to the creek and was riding bareback with a rope round his neck, he took it into his head to get excited and canter along the road ; and as I was not able to stop him (not having a bridle), I simply let him go and held on tight. After breakfast this morning we had to go and head some steers, and got back about half-past one.

I can harness a pair of horses, and put them in a rig now almost without a mistake. The canaries here fly about in flocks just as sparrows with you, and there are some splendid butterflies and humming-birds.

Three days ago we began taking in the hay here; the work is not at all unpleasant, but rather hard. We had breakfast at six a.m., dinner at twelve, tea in the field or lawn, supper at nine. Yesterday we went on working till nine, so as to be able to have a picnic to-morrow up the mountain. I was awfully glad to get to bed, but was all right this morning. I was down at ten, just in time for breakfast, as I did not have to fetch the cows in at six as usual. Of course everywhere people have to work late with the hay when there is fear of rain, and there is a certain amount of fun in hurrying it in, as those in the field try to put on the loads so as to race those who are unloading at the barn. This is really very exciting. I have been at the barn stowing the hay away as it is brought. The weather is delightful, not too warm, with a cool breeze from the lake, though a few days ago it was awfully hot (96° in the shade). The mosquitoes are gradually disappearing, and that is a good thing.

Sundays here are very jolly, as there is no work to do except occasionally to herd cattle ; and that cannot be called work, as we sit in a shady place and read, and have a dog to look after the beasts.

July.—As you may like to have a more accurate account of our work, here is an extract from my diary :

Saturday.

Up at six a.m. Watered and groomed Tiny, and cleaned out his stable ; milked two cows, and fed the calves. They eat like little pigs. At eight, breakfast. After breakfast harnessed Tiny to the buggy ;

fetched the sheep down for one to be killed, and then took them back. After dinner herded cattle up beyond the old farm. There were heaps of wild strawberries and raspberries. Brought the cattle back at five, had a bathe, and milked two cows.

Monday.

Up at six a.m., and bathed the foreleg of the mare with hot water ; also had to milk her, as the colt was not allowed to go near her. Then did some hoeing in the garden, and had a bathe. After breakfast and dinner did a lot of various little jobs.

Tuesday.

Up at six a.m., and milked the mare again. Shifted some pea-straw out of the barn. After breakfast unloaded a waggon of hay, and got very hot, as we were in a hurry expecting another load, which, by the way, never came. In the afternoon we played a lawn-tennis match with the B—— Club. Herbert and I won both our doubles and singles. I played the captain, who said he had not been beaten for three years.

When I was running the horse-rake the other day, I had a slight shine or two with Lucy, who was in the rake. Once she reared up and nearly broke the shaft, which brought the 'boss' round to see what was up in pretty quick time.

Yesterday I got up at six as usual, and after a piece of bread-and-butter was set to work at some weeding in the garden (I usually go and fetch the cows). It had been raining all the day before, and during the night too. The clothes I wore were: large straw hat, flannel shirt, pair of blue serge trousers, socks, and top-boots. At eight o'clock I came in to breakfast, which consisted of ham, tea, bread-and-butter. After breakfast I went out and picked raspberries (growing on canes or bushes about two feet six inches high). This I did till twelve ; my back was then beginning to ache. We then had dinner, which lasted about half an hour. I picked more raspberries till two p.m. Afterwards I helped Herbert put a team of colts into the carriage, and we went off to play a tennis-match at C——. The day I have just described was one which we should term decidedly easy, as we generally have not to pick fruit except when there is a large supply wanted. Another reason was that it had been raining off and on for the last week, and thus delayed the haying, which had just begun. We found that hard work, and no mistake. Three days ago we had a picnic to the shores of the Georgian Bay. We bathed and ate wild strawberries, and enjoyed ourselves very much. The roads here are awfully rough : now and then they are varied by patches of corduroy roads, which consist of trunks of trees. This makes a good deal of bumping.

July.—I have only time for a few words. We have been getting in hay very fast. On Wednesday there was a sudden and very severe rainstorm. I only brought in a load of hay about three minutes before it was raining bucketfuls; and then the wind got up suddenly, and one of the men had to rush and shut the barn-doors to prevent the roof being blown off. On Friday and Saturday we were working at hay till half-past eight. To-morrow, Monday, we begin the wheat harvest. I expect we shall have a fairly busy time of it. We had an upset driving a team of colts into C—— on Wednesday. One of them shied at a log in the road, and we were all quietly deposited in the ditch. Nobody was hurt.

August.—We have just finished taking the hay in here, and for the next month or two we shall be employed getting in the harvest; that means breakfast at six, and work till eight or nine in the evening.

We began cutting the wheat yesterday with a new machine that cuts the wheat and binds it into sheaves. All the hay-season I have worked in the barns, taking the hay from the waggons and putting it away, which is hot and dusty work, though I have got used to it by now.

I feed the calves every morning and evening with pails of milk, and most exasperating they are. As there are four calves and two pails, three of them get to one pail and one to the other; the consequence is that the three get their heads jammed in and then jump about.

We have several colts here. I am learning to ride them bareback, sometimes without a bridle and with only a rope round their necks. I can manage to stick on now, though not very comfortably. I have only been chucked off once. Three nights ago we had a tremendous thunderstorm. I was wakened about twenty minutes to three by the bedclothes being lifted off me by the wind (we sleep with both door and window open). There was only just time to get up and shut the window, when the rain came down in torrents. The lightning was wonderfully bright and incessant. Once I could read my watch for nearly five minutes consecutively.

CHAPTER III.

Harvesting.—An Awkward Customer.—A Hot Corner.
—How to Drive in the Dark.—Finishing the Grain
Harvest.

August.—To-day being Sunday, we had breakfast at a quarter-past ten, though I have been
up since seven, as I had to look after the
driving horses, and wanted to have time for a
bathe as well. Dick has been out most of
the morning, and is now herding cattle. He
has to drive them to the pastures and then
watch them to prevent their getting to the
crops. We have been very busy all this
week cutting the wheat and barley and then
stacking it up. Yesterday Dick and W——
played a tennis match against O——, beating
them very easily indeed. We do not expect

to have any spare time for the next month, as we shall be bringing in the different crops. There has just been a spell of cool weather ; but it is hot again now—about 96°. By this time I can manage to stick on to a horse bareback pretty tight. This morning we took three horses to the creek to water, and raced back. We had only bridles on, so it was rather exciting.

We are both well, and so sunburnt that I don't think you would know us if you met us in our working dress—a large straw hat, a gray shirt, an old pair of trousers, and sometimes boots up to the knees, the sleeves of the shirts generally rolled up to the elbows, our arms, hands, and faces being just about the colour of the chess-box which Aunt K—— gave us. Tell B—— that he would be surprised to see the way they garden here ; the celery trench is a slight furrow, made with the corner of a hoe, $1\frac{1}{2}$ inches deep ; and the tomatoes are planted out in patches like cabbages. I don't think the fruit here is much better than at home—the gooseberries are not nearly so good ; they have, however, a very good kind of red currant, called the ' cherry currant '; the berries are about as big round as a fourpenny-bit, perhaps a little larger. M—— wants to know how we get on without ices. I expect we eat a good many more than you do. We never go into C—— without having nearly a dozen each. Every-one you meet treats you to an ice or lemonade. Dick sends S—— a letter on birch-bark. It is just the same as they make the canoes from, the rough outside skin being peeled off with a knife.

August.—All last week we have been get-ting in the wheat. We have worked from 6.30 till 12 and from 1 till 8 or 9—good long hours, and heaps to do the whole time. Yesterday I went to the boss's other farm, about six miles off, to give a hand there. Over twenty acres of wheat passed through my hands, or rather through my pitchfork. I pitched ten loads of sheaves on to the waggons, and then pitched four loads off—all between 12.30 and 7.30— and then I was less tired than on any other evening this week. We shall have got the whole of the wheat and barley in by Tuesday night. You ask about tobacco and cigars here. They are simply ghastly. As for the fauna and flora, they are nothing very great. There are squirrels, musk-rats, mice, chip- munks (a sort of half-squirrel), ground-hogs (a sort of prairie-dog, I suppose, about three feet long), minx, polecat, and, very seldom, a skunk; garter-snakes; and one or two rattle- snakes are seen every year. A few humming- birds, lots of canaries, sparrows, and robins (a kind of red-breasted thrush), blackbirds (a kind of small crow), crows, and lots of small birds of the lark and stone-chat kind. The flowers are rather poor, the wild iris being the best.

August.—We have been harvesting in real earnest—following a reaping-machine and stacking up the sheaves into groups of ten (each consists of two leaning against each other). This I did the other day from 6.45 a.m. till 7 p.m. — ten acres, about. I could not work fast as there was a high wind on. At other times we have been unloading waggon-loads of sheaves in a barn. This is done with hay-forks; the sheaves have to be tossed sometimes ten feet above your head, to somebody who catches them with a fork, and then throws them to another fellow who shoves them away. I have done most of the unloading here, and find it requires good muscles as well as a certain knack. Yesterday I pitched off loads of sheaves from 6.30 a.m. till 9 p.m., allowing intervals for meals; the only parts of me at all stiff were my fingers. This shows that I am getting pretty well hardened to the work. I think the harvesting very jolly, and

I am seldom really tired now after a day of it. This morning, Sunday, I went down with P. B—— to herd cattle about half-past eight. We came back at ten minutes to eleven. I was rather hungry, as I had not had anything to eat since yesterday's tea at 4.30. We have very fine cucumbers here, and plenty of them. I ate one about thirteen inches long for breakfast this morning. The weather now is hot enough to roast a potato.

August.—We have at last got all the wheat in, and on Friday we had our first threshing, from six a.m. till six p.m., with one hour's stop for dinner at twelve. Dick was in the wheat-mow handing (or rather forking) out sheaves, and I had charge of two colts in the straw-mow, and had to drive them round to tramp down the straw. They had tremendously hard work, and were so tired that they did not resist at all when we rolled them out of a hole at the top of the barn on to a heap of straw. I thought they would never get down safe, but they did somehow. We got the straw packed in so tight that the sides of the barn bulged out considerably. About 500 bushels of wheat were threshed out of fifty acres—not very grand, was it? The boss has been keeping a thorough-bred polled Angus cow for his brothers. It is a great job milking it, as it kicks like one o'clock. It has to have its hind legs roped together, and then it jumps around pretty lively. As it weighs over 1,500 pounds, you may imagine what a business it is. It has a calf, and charges round in very lively style on every opportunity. It will run half a mile to get at a dog. The other day it nearly knocked a colt through the stable wall. Horned cattle are the only things which it is afraid of, never having had anything to do with them before. I have told you that the housewives have come in very useful. So would the looking-glass also on the railway journey, if I had but had a pocket-comb with me. As it was, I could only see the state I was in without being able to remedy it. About half of the harvesting is done now. Oats and barley are being brought in. Three days ago, when it was raining, we put all the wheat that had been threshed through a fanning-mill to separate it from the chaff, grass-seeds, etc. I had to supply the mill, and it kept me going pretty sharp. The quantity of house-flies is positively awful. They are most irritating and injurious to the temper. The heat is fearful. I write this letter in my shirt-sleeves, gasping for breath at every word, and the perspiration pouring down my face into my eyes, and maddening me almost as much as the flies do. The pigs of the establishment have been put in my charge. At present there are ten, but I expect many more. Two are being prepared for exhibition, and eight for fattening.

September.—We are still hard at work harvesting, and shall continue to be till the end of this month. On Thursday and Friday we were threshing barley and wheat. The dust was something awful. Not getting the wheat done in one day, we started again the next, and in the afternoon did a full hour's work in thirty-five minutes. The machine-men were rushing it. My place was at the end of the straw-carrier. Dick was next. I passed it to him at the rate of thirty forkfulls a minute, and he kept pace, but the man next him could not, and a great pile rose up next Dick, compelling him to fork higher, and so I had to pass the straw higher too. We built a stack twelve yards long by six yards broad and about twelve feet high in the thirty-five minutes, the whole passing through first my hands and then Dick's. On Monday P. B—— and I drove twenty miles to a place where we had business. We walked the horses the whole way there, as we had a cow tied on behind. We started at eleven a.m., and got there at half-past eight, with an hour's stop halfway. After something to eat, we started back again at ten p.m., this time without the cow. But after we had gone a couple of miles we had to stop, as it was so dark that we could not see over the horses' ears. I made my way to a neighbouring farmhouse, which we could see by its light, and fell into a ditch and ran into two fences before I got there. I bought a lantern for fifty cents and returned. I found we had driven right across the road, and that the horses were standing in a large ditch about three feet deep. So, you see, we only stopped just in time. The only way we had of driving before we got the light was to go as straight as we could till we felt the side wheels of the buggy going down into the ditch, and then to pull the horses a little the other way till we felt the other ditch. We hung the lantern on the dash-board of the carriage, and started again. By its light we could see about two yards ahead of the horses. We got home about eight next morning, both very sleepy. All yesterday I was following a self-binding reaper setting up the sheaves. As the thistles were plentiful my hand became rather like a pincushion full of pins. On Wednesday I bought some common cotton shirts to work in when barley had to be couched, as the beards stick into the flannel ones and make them feel like hair-shirts. The flannel our shirts were made of was too good, and the perspiration made them shrink awfully at first ; they ought to have been of much coarser flannel.

September.—It would be very nice if you could send me a drawing of Neighbour's new hive. From what you say it seems to be handy, and would indeed suit this climate very well. It is extraordinary how few people keep bees here, though they would have splendid honey-getting facilities, as there are two crops of clover and heaps of wild raspberries, and bushes of that kind. You will be glad to hear that we have nearly finished getting in the harvest. Indeed, after this week I do not think there will be any more working after six in the evening. We shall have, I think, about three days, and that will about end up everything except the root-crops, and they only take about a week to get in. Now, as to wearing something when barley-threshing, I find that it is not anything like so bad as represented. The last time we threshed barley I had two hours in what is supposed to be the worst place, and I found no inconvenience at all. (I took the place while the man who had it went to get a drink, and then found it was not worth while to go back to my old station.) But, anyhow, I shall get some goggles. They are better than veils, which it would be impossible to wear—one gets quite hot enough without them. There is no danger of our over-working ourselves, as we generally manage to get into a place where nobody can run us. I have been only tired out once since I came here ; I had to do some very heavy pitching. I pitched eight loads of wheat-sheaves over a beam seven feet high and sixteen feet behind me, and further had to keep pace with the man who pitched them off the waggon. I managed to hurry the man who took the straw from me. I did not feel the least tired about an hour afterwards, when I had had a bathe. Yesterday afternoon I was running a mowing-machine, rigged up so as to cut peas. I rather liked it, after stacking sheaves of barley and oats.

Perhaps you would like to know something of our regular expenses here : Three dollars a month for washing, some postage, a missionary subscription, and one or two other small things, so you see we do not need much. What we spend the money on is chiefly those things we were not able to bring out or did not know of. I think it would be worth while almost to send you the flannel shirts we have not used, or get rid of them, as it is ruin to them to use them and have them washed here. We could get some more suitable ones in their place. The Parcel Post is thirty-five cents a pound for anything under five pounds.

CHAPTER IV.

A Slight Relaxation.—The Indian Summer.—Getting in the Root Crops.—What ought to be Learnt before Coming to Canada.

September.—This week we began drawing in peas, of which there are fifty acres. I had to level it, straw and all, and tramp it down. This was very warm and dusty work. Sometimes I sank down into it three or four feet deep ; I rather liked it, as there was some satisfaction in seeing a heap about eight feet high trampled down quite level, for it is very soft. The waggons were unloaded in four forkfuls, the fork being worked by horse-power, and fastened on pulleys. On Tuesday morning I herded cattle. It was awfully hot, so I drove them down close to the bush, and, getting into the shade, went to sleep. The cattle did the same, so I had an easy time of it. In the afternoon I helped to stow away sheaves of barley in the barn. In the evening we all drove to a ball in C—— and had a jolly time. We came back the same night, arriving at half-past two. Next morning we got up at seven, worked till breakfast at eight, and then went to tramp peas and stow oats. Before breakfast on Saturday I was half-way home from the stream, where I had been watering a colt, when a train came running along the line, which is about ten yards from the road ; the colt shied, and threw me off on to my head. I got a goodish cut on it, but nothing more happened, except that I was stunned for about a minute. After dinner I fished in the stream. At first I used grass-hoppers for bait, with shot or float ; I got a few small ones this way. The biggest I got by using only a piece of pink string. On Friday

night we went to another ball at C——,
which was rather a big affair. There were
about forty people there. The woods about
here are now beginning to change. The
Virginian creeper has turned a deep red, and
looks splendid as it hangs down from the
trees.

October.—There was an exhibition in C——
a week ago. A number of prizes were offered
for exhibits of honey and wax. Only one man
exhibited, and his exhibit seemed to us a very
poor affair. The 1-lb. sections could not have
weighed more than 10 oz. each. The exhibition was very good for a town the size of
C——. There was a splendid show of fruit,
especially apples, some of which weighed a
pound apiece. Mrs. B—— showed fruit,
vegetables, flowers, and poultry, getting in all
seventeen prizes—ten or eleven firsts. Nothing
from the farm was shown, though they had intended to show two pigs ; but it would have

taken too much trouble. We have been having some wet and cold weather lately, and there was a heavy fall of snow on Friday; but we hope to get three weeks of fine weather —the Indian summer—before the cold sets in. There were three inches of snow on the ground at mid-day ; it was considered unusually early, as they seldom have a fall till the middle of this month, and not often then. The wild duck and geese are beginning to come, though we have had no shooting to speak of yet ; we hope to get some soon. Dick and I preserve skins of anything which we shoot. The woods are looking splendid now. Imagine Virginian creepers hanging down from trees some three or four hundred feet high. On Wednesday we had a football match at C——. I played for them, and we won by three goals to one. I don't think that I ever looked forward to Sundays so much as I do now. The only work which we have to do is to feed the pigs. After breakfast to-day I strolled down to the creek and caught a few fish. Then came lunch. After lunch a pleasing repose. The rest of the family all went to Sunday-school, excepting the 'boss;' so he and I cooked the dinner. Towards the end of this month Dick and I hope to go camping on the islands in the lake and get a little shooting. There is not much game to be got round about here.

October.—The last three or four days have been splendid ; the Indian summer has regularly set in. We have been busy carting in peas and oats ; it is rather late to do so, but the rainy weather we have had threw us back very much. We work now till 6.30; by that time it is nearly dark. There will be a tremendous rush for the next fortnight, getting in the root crops and finishing the harvest. After this there cannot be much more to do, except preparing for the winter. This morning, after feeding the pigs, horses, etc., I went with

P—— in the 'buggy' to look for the sheep which had strayed away in the road. We started at 8.15 and got back at 11, driving about fourteen miles over roads filled with mudholes, often quite a foot deep, and in places covered with boulders. Last night I went with P——, driving round the country. He was buying up cockerels to fatten for the winter; he gave 20 or 25 cents (about 10d. or 1s.) a pair for them. Turkeys can be bought from 60 to 75 or 80 cents; geese for 45 cents. Still poultry are said to pay pretty well here.

The wild geese and duck are coming down from the North in large numbers now; the flocks of geese sometimes numbering as many as a hundred. We are trying to rush the harvest, and shall get it done in three days if the weather holds fine. There are huge quantities of fruit going now; the grapes are ripe; and there is such a quantity of apples that they are lying by hundreds on the ground, where they rot for want of eating. We do all we can to save waste ; but we can't manage more than twenty apples each in one day besides the grapes. Out here it seems the more fruit you eat the better your health is; at least, we find it so. Dances at C—— are coming on now. I have been learning the Canadian dances, and am getting quite clever at them.

October.—Snow has been lying on the ground for the last three days. Last night we had quite a hard frost, and to-day there have been snow, hail, and rain off and on. On Thursday Dick went to S—— (a town nine miles off) helping a man to drive some cattle which he bought from the boss ; he walked back, as he did not care to wait five hours for the next train. When he got in, the whole front of his waterproof was a sheet of ice, from the sleet and hail ; however, he did not get a bit wet, as he had boots up to his knees, and a waterproof down to his ankles. We have just finished getting in the apples and grapes; we were only just in time to save them from the frost. On Tuesday I went to a party in C——; we got there about 8.30, which was in good time, considering that we only stopped work at half-past six, and had to dress, have tea, and drive five miles. Dick could not go, as he had a cold. All tennis is over now; we shall get no more warm weather. We have taken to chess instead. How does K——'s cow do? Do you know that the usual cost of a first-class cow here, except, of course, 'thoroughbreds,' is $20? A good horse costs from $100 to $200, which is very little compared with what is given in England. Of course they are not quite such good ones. I milk the five cows every morning and evening now; one of them kicks furiously. Yesterday afternoon we had a great time putting up the stoves. They have no regular fireplaces here, but a stove in one of the lower rooms; a pipe runs up through the ceiling into a bedroom, and then into the chimney, and thus warms both rooms splendidly. There is only one coal-stove in the house, and that is in the hall; it is a ' self-feeder ;' the hopper only has to be filled morning and night, and then it feeds the fire by itself. Everyone here seems to feel the cold tremendously, though it only seems just a little cool to Dick and myself. They say that Englishmen never do feel it half so much the first few winters.

We are still working at the root crops—grubbing up potatoes with our hands after the plough has been over the lines. We also have to grub up mangolds and slice the tops off. This work, which we have kept up for two or three days running, is somewhat hard on the back and hands. To-day we went to the B—— Farm, four miles off, and cleaned barley in a fanning mill. When we drove home again, the teamster went as hard as he could over the 'corduroy' bridges and the stones. The jolting was something appalling, and we had to hang on with our eyelids, thanking our stars that it was not after tea. I have gained 5½ lb. in three weeks. During the harvest-time I weighed 153 lb., now I weigh 158½ lb. —just what I did when I left the old country. We are told that during the winter we shall get very fat.

October.—You ask what knowledge will be of use to you if you join us out here. There are plenty of things which you might learn with advantage—carpentering and blacksmithing, for instance ; but a little veterinary knowledge would be worth all the rest put together. It is of the very greatest importance out here, as everybody has something to do with cattle, and hardly any have any veterinary knowledge. I only wish we had been able to learn something of it before we came out. As it is, we shall have to read it up now as much as we

can. Thatching and gardening are also good
things to know something about. Dick's
fall was not the first, and will not be the last.
I have been thrown off about fifteen or twenty
times already—indeed, I am getting quite used
to it now. We shall have a lot of driving
and riding this winter, as there will be several
horses to be exercised. The life out here is
pretty much what we expected, perhaps rather
more civilized. The country has a most
quaint appearance after England. For instance, in pretty nearly every field are large
piles of wood, stones, etc., and now and then
the tall charred trunk of a tree quite bare of
limbs, and burnt into the most extraordinary
shapes. Another curious feature in the
country is the roads, if we may so call them.
You drive over them in a waggon without
springs, sitting on a board or anything that
comes handy. This, as you may imagine, is
the very extreme of all that is annoying and
painful. Bringing in the root-crops is perhaps

the most unpleasant work : harvesting, though hard enough, is rather jolly. We shall have some ploughing soon. There is a nice piece of rough ground reserved specially for us, and it looks very inviting, as it has only lately been cleared. We don't get much shooting, as on a big farm like this there is generally something to do. This time I'm afraid we shall not be able to get any camping-out, since the weather has made us late with the root crops. They will not be done till the end of this month. The mangolds and potatoes are done, but there still remain about 12,000 bushels of turnips to be brought in. This morning we all drove down to church, Dick and I in the buggy. The others started ahead of us, and when we tried to pass kept galloping across the road in front of us. Tiny got so excited that I could not hold him, and he ran away. We passed them then sure enough, but there was a corner just in front, which we went round at full speed. I made sure we

should have been upset, as the outside wheels
of the buggy were quite two feet from the
ground, and there is a steep hill the other side
of the corner.   However, I managed to stop
him.   But when we got to the bridge we had
more trouble.   Some people who had been
celebrating Hallowe'en had put a big red
waggon on the railing on one side and a large
sleigh on the other.   Of course Tiny would
not pass these at first, and when he did he
had his front legs in the air most of the time.
We got down just in time for church.

CHAPTER V.

November.—The winter is really commencing
now. A day or two ago we had quite a hard
frost; the water-jugs in two of the rooms were
frozen, and the cold kept on during the whole
of the next day. Last Saturday week a sudden
snowstorm came on while we were pulling
turnips. It was so thick that you could not
see a team of horses forty yards away. As it
was impossible to leave the turnips which we
had been pulling to be frozen while lying on
the ground, we had to go on at it. All hands

were started to load them on to the carts and waggons. This was somewhat cold for the fingers. Fortunately the storm only lasted half an hour. Still, it left an inch and a half of snow on the ground. By the way, if not too late, the woollen gloves should be like babies' gloves—a big bag for the fingers and a small one for the thumb ; those with fingers are next door to useless.

I got your letter on Tuesday at dinner ; but had not time to read it as I had to go to a threshing. We were having a great time threshing just then ; it lasted all Monday, Tuesday, and Wednesday. We began at seven on Monday, and threshed out one barn on that day. As it is best not to wash the face in the middle of a threshing, we did not wash for dinner, and so looked as black as niggers. The only clean place on the face was just round the mouth, where we had to make a road for the provisions. Washing the face makes the dust stick worse.

On Wednesday we finished the second barn and started on another ; I was outside on the stack while it was raining, snowing, hailing, and blowing. At twelve I drove a man home who had hurt himself a bit. As I went straight from the threshing, and was wet through when I came back, I had a thick coat of mud all over. In the afternoon Dick was on the stack while I went on horseback to return a lot of sacks which had been lent to the 'boss.' When I got back the threshing was over. As they had threshed a few peas the dust was very bad. Dick, when he came in, had a quarter of an inch of solid mud all over his face, and I had to scrape part of it off with his knife before he washed. The mud consisted of chaff, barley-beards, and dust. He began with goggles on, but they got caked over at once. It freezes every night now, and sometimes in the day. The other day it started to freeze about 10 a.m., after quite a mild night. Dick and I have

bought some felt overshoes, which go over
light shoes such as we brought out, and are
much warmer than boots ; they are also snow-
proof. The soles and sides are of india-rubber.
They will last at least two winters. Every-
one here wears them, and you can go out to
work with only a pair of slippers and these
overshoes on in the coldest weather. We
don't have such early hours now as in the
summer ; we seldom get up before 6.30 or 7.

Our winter has not begun in earnest yet ;
it is most unusually late. The last thing that
we have done is moving the large straw-stacks,
formed during the threshing, into barns. This
finished yesterday, thank goodness! and thus
ends the regular work. Cattle-feeding has
just begun ; that is, we get up at 6.30 and
give the cattle some food to last till we have
had our breakfast. Then they get turnips
sliced up by a machine, which we have to
turn—and pretty stiff work it is. Afterwards
they are watered, the whole stable is cleaned

out, and the beasts are bedded down with clean straw. This takes about an hour and a half, and has to be done every morning and evening, Sundays included. Dick feeds the pigs (fifteen of them), and I look after the horses, so we do not come in for the cattle work much. You will be pleased to hear that Dick weighs 11 stone 9, and is increasing. He was 10 stone 10 a month ago. I am also in good condition, but I should not like to say how much my weight is.

December.—Dick and I have been staying with B—— in Toronto for a few days. When we left B—— there was a foot and a half of snow on the ground, and we were quite prepared to spend the night in the train. The first train took one hour to do the three miles between B—— and C——. It had two engines and only two cars. However, we were only an hour late, taking six and a half hours to do

ninety miles. We had had a snowstorm during
the whole of the two days before we left, and
it was just clearing a little when we did leave.
On the day before we left we had a shooting-
match, which was almost extinguished by the
snow. We had to stand inside a building and
shoot at a mark outside. There were only
four turkeys competed for, and I got two and
Dick one; we paid ten cents apiece for shots,
and we each had three shots. We sold the
turkeys to Mrs. B—— for fifty cents apiece.
The long boots which we brought out here
are splendid. I spent two days walking about
in snow, sometimes three or four feet deep,
and my feet never got damp. By loosening
the laces, too, we can make them quite warm.
The corduroy trousers are also very warm.
I expect when you receive this letter you will
be making preparations for the Christmas
dinner, such as stirring the plum-pudding, etc.
We were back at B—— in time to help in
the big stir. I was cutting up beef five or

six days ago, and I cut a round weighing over thirty pounds to be spiced for Christmas. Do you know I am getting quite an expert butcher now ; I can cut up a beef quicker than you could believe. When we returned to B—— we found that our work had become much easier. Sawing and splitting wood, feeding horses and cattle, and sleigh-driving were our chief occupations. As yet we have had no snow-shoeing or skating. But the sleighing is simply splendid : you go along so smoothly, with a light, swinging motion, and as it is cold, you are able to let the horses go at full speed without their getting hot. You asked in your last letter about white foxes. Once or twice they have come down as far as here, but very seldom. There are minx, however, and plenty of partridges and rabbits. Everything now is in a state of great preparation for Christmas. Three great rounds of beef are being spiced in the cellar. In the evening we go and help decorate the church. As there is no holly here, all the decorations are in swamp cedar, a tree which looks something like an arbor vitæ. The sleighing is very good now, though the snow is only four inches deep. Lately we have been doing some teaming. Dick has charge of one team and I of another. We have great fun sometimes when there are a lot of boys round. They run and try to get on to the back of the sleigh, and then we either go so fast as to prevent them getting on or swing them off going round the corners. The sleighs are built like this

The top of the sleigh is constructed so as to turn on the runners, so that when you go sharply round a corner the back runners swing right round and run out to one side for a few moments. It is almost impossible then to

hold on to it.   Here is a sketch of the position of a sleigh turning a corner.

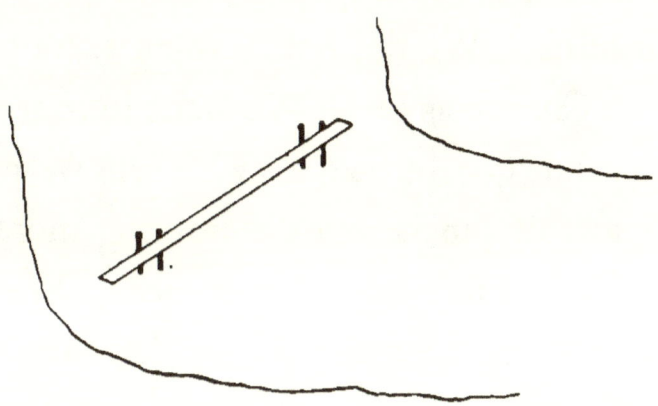

December.—It was snowing hard all day here on Christmas Eve.   During the morning and the best part of the afternoon the snow was very soft and wetting.   We got nearly wet through —the only things that did not let in the wet were the corduroys.   However, about half-past four it began to freeze ferociously, and one's coat got as hard as a board and crackled when one moved one's arms about.   When I brought my team into the stable they were covered with snow and ice nearly an inch thick, and I had to scrape it off with a large knife used for topping turnips. That night the six o'clock train passed B—— at twelve, having been snowed up at a place, thirty miles south of us. We did not have an extra great time on Christmas Day. We went in to service at 11 and got out at 2.15 ; then we had a small sort of lunch, and did nothing more till 5.30, when there was a great feed. We had no work to do that day, as we had arranged with the man who does most of the feeding that we should give him a goose, and he should do all the work ; he proposed it, and we were very glad to accept his offer. Thank you very much for the *Graphic* and *Illustrated.* The pictures will very nearly finish covering the walls of our room, which are half covered already. We have got some really heavy snow here now, and some pretty bad drifts. Last evening, about 5.30, T—— and I started in the cutter—a single horse sleigh to hold two or three—to fetch P——from a place four miles from here. We had nearly arrived there when

we got off the beaten track—it was snowing
so hard that I had to let the horse take his
own way, and trust to his keeping on the
track—and in less than half a minute we went
slap into a deep drift. The horse and cutter
stopped dead, and when we got out the snow
was just up to our arm-pits and I could only
see part of the horse's neck and his head. As
we had lightened the cutter by getting out,
the horse managed to pull it through the
drift, and we started again with our pockets
and clothes stuffed full of snow. When we came
back we managed to keep what little track
there was, but we had to walk the horse most
of the way. This morning six more inches of
snow had fallen when we woke ; fortunately
there was no wind, but if it does blow at all
the roads will be nearly impassable.

We are getting some pretty severe frosts now,
and F—— has already had occasion to have
his nose rubbed with snow. We are wearing jerseys over our shirts and under our

waistcoats, and when it gets really cold we shall start vests and cardigans too. We have had one or two small blizzards. I wish we could let one loose, by way of effect, on our friends at home—they would never want another dose. They are truly awful things. The snow freezes in great lumps on your eyebrows and chin and nose—every now and then you have to use your hands to open your eyes, which get frozen up. It is quite impossible to keep the snow from getting down your neck. Dick is getting horribly fat and lazy. Every evening, nearly, when he sits down in the sitting-room, he goes to sleep and snores loudly. The Misses B—— generally wake him up by dropping the cat on to his face, or something of that kind.

January, 1887.—You are right in thinking it cold here; on Thursday the thermometer was at 15° F. all day. I wore a cap in the morning, but in the afternoon a hood showing only my eyes and nose. My breath condensed into a lump of ice half as big as my fist on the outside of the hood. It was impossible to keep always at work—about every ten minutes you had to stop, and start jumping up and down and bang your arms round to get warm again. Even the milk got frozen in carrying it from the stables to the house, a distance of about 150 yards. Ever since Thursday night we have had a terrific blizzard blowing. The snow is now three feet on the level, and runs up to ten or fifteen feet in the drifts.

Yesterday, Dick, F——, and I were in the pleasure sleigh. We got into a drift, and broke three out of four traces. In the afternoon we started to go to C——, and took an hour and a half to go a little over a mile. Then we got into a drift and stuck completely, the snow being over the horses' backs. They were quite unable to move either themselves or the sleigh, so we got out. It looked most peculiar to see each one, as he got out, sink

right down to his arm-pits, and his great loose
ulster spread out on the snow alongside. We
trampled the snow down by the horses, then
lifted the sleigh right round and went back.
When we arrived at home our faces were caked
over with frozen snow, leaving only a space
for eyes and nose.

All to-day they have been running single
engines, with snow-ploughs, on the railway
track to keep it open. No one thought the
clergyman would be able to get here this
morning from D——, five miles off, but he
did so, arriving at about twelve. He had
taken over three hours, and had to walk in
front of his horse and sleigh most of the way.
Of course there was no congregation, so he
went back.

January.—We are not having nearly such
cold weather now as before. Generally there
are only about 20° of frost during the day, and
32° at night. Whereas we have been having

6° or 8° below zero during the day, and 19° or 20° below at night.

I will now proceed to gratify your heart by telling you what I am wearing. On cold days (8° below zero) I wear vest, pants, corduroys, flannel shirt, jersey, waistcoat or cardigan, and leather-trimmed jacket, high boots, one pair of socks, a pair of wool mitts, a pair of buck-skins, and a cap. This cap we only pull right over our faces during blizzards. On comparatively warm days I wear the same, minus the cardigan or waistcoat.

The work now consists in getting up at 6.30 or 7, grooming our respective teams of horses; then breakfast at 7.30, the whole crowd of us together, eleven in all. After breakfast I feed the pigs; then we harness our teams and draw chaff, hay, turnips, or carrots from the barn, or from pits in the fields, as the case may be. It is rather fun driving to the fields, for in front of the gateway and all round it there is a large drift. When the horses see this they make for it as hard as they can, plunging and jumping in fine style in the snow, which is often up to their backs. Sometimes they get in so deep that we have to drag their legs out, or the sleigh, or both —standing up to our waists to do it. After dinner we do the same till 5.20; then we take the horses to water, feed pigs, colts, etc., knock the snow and ice off their feet, and come in about 6.30 and have tea.

It is, great fun to see the steam snow-ploughs pass here on the railroad; they come past at full speed, and run full tilt into a drift which is often as high as the smoke-stack. After a short time, amid a tremendous cloud of snow, you see the plough appearing on the other side perfectly choked up with snow. It has cut clean through the drift, leaving a high wall on either side. Sometimes they have to charge two or three times at a drift before they can cut through it. The passenger-trains are often several hours late.

February.—A few days ago P—— and I drove to Mr. L——'s to see a friend, who has got work there. Mr. L—— is supposed to have the best stables north of Toronto. They are certainly very nice, and it is very easy to feed cattle and horses in them. Here it takes one man the whole day to feed thirty head, while there one man in an hour and a half can do all that is necessary in the morning, and the same at night. Our friend seemed to like his quarters very much. He gets $5 a month and his board, and in the summer he is to get $10. The other day I had a great time driving a cow down here from North L——. I think that I mentioned in a letter about the end of September that P—— and I took a cow there. Well, I had to fetch it back. I started at 7 a.m., and walked six miles to the railway track. I caught the train at S——, which brought me to North L—— about 9.30. I then went and got the cow at once and started to lead it back home, a dis-

tance of some twenty miles. As it had been
kept in the stable and fed very well since
September, it was exceedingly lively, and,
indeed, during the first five hundred yards,
rolled me over three times in the snow.
After that, however, it cooled down, and
walked along quietly for the first four miles.
Then it got tired, and I had to pull it along
by the halter ; it was terribly slow, as the
snow prevented us from going more than two
miles an hour. I got very hungry before we
got to S——, the first place where we could
stop. This we reached at about 2.30. After
three-quarters of an hour for food and rest,
both for myself and the cow and its calf—for
it had a calf—we started on again. The cow
was still tired, and the calf rather footsore, so
it was a slow business. About half-way there
the cow stopped dead and refused to move an
inch. I was just wondering what on earth I
should do when a man came along with three
calves which he had brought from S——,

starting an hour after I did. With his help I managed to get them the rest of the way, though it was anything but easy work. The cow was a very valuable animal, a thorough-bred polled Angus, worth $200. Three days ago we had another blizzard, which left us another foot of snow. To-day the thermometer stands at 10° below zero, but there is no wind, and the sun is very hot and the sky as blue as in summer. Last night we went to a political meeting. The two candidates had both called a meeting at the same place and at the same time. Of course there was a row. They both set to work to abuse each other. At last the Liberal had to go, as things were getting a little too hot for him.

In your last letter you asked more particularly about the sport here. We might have got some very decent deer-hunting if we had had time. Two or three fellows from the neighbourhood made a camping-out expedition to the mouth of the Nottawasage River,

not very far from here. They had a
great time, and shot several deer. Quite a
number of wild-duck and a few gangs of
geese came in October and November ; but
as they were very wild, and everybody was
out after them, it was not easy to get a shot.
The fish to be obtained in the Georgian Bay
are ' black bass,' which are caught with a
spoon and give plenty of play ; ' white-fish,'
the same as pike, to judge by appearance, and
caught in the same way. There are also
plenty of lake-trout. Occasionally people
use flies for these ; but most of the fish, I'm
sorry to say, are taken with nets. In the
mill-streams and rivers there are plenty of
chub. For these I usually bait with a grass-
hopper.

And now I wish to tell you something of
our plans for going North-West in the spring.
When in Toronto we asked the advice both
of Colonel D—— and the G——. They
both said it was the best thing we could do.

Calgary in Alberta is where we specially thought of going. It is just east of the Rockies, and the climate is very much milder than here. We thought of spending two years there, and then, if it still seemed advisable, of going on to British Columbia. We could then decide which of the three we liked best, before settling down for good—British Columbia, the North-West, or Ontario. This we must do at once, as all free land grants are to cease in 1890 ; though probably the time will be extended. As to getting there, we shall try and get a passage with some cattle. Men taking cattle up there employ several men to look after them, and give them free passes over the railway. If we cannot manage this, we shall, of course, have to pay our fare, which will be $50 by immigrant-car. We should have to have about $25 in our pockets when we got there. Altogether we should want about $125—twenty-five pounds. Once there, we shall board ourselves if we can. That will be cheaper than boarding out at $12 a month. Of course the man with whom we get work may give us board and lodging as well as wages. But if we board ourselves we can do something in the way of keeping bees, poultry, and a cow. I dare say the cooking would not be good at first, but practice will improve that. It would require some outlay to start this, about $10 ; but we should more than get this back in six months' time. We feel that the sooner we learn to do for ourselves the better it will be. We can get a shanty for $1 50 cents per month.

T——— seems to be learning quite the right kind of things in England. Horse-shoeing he will find most useful ; I only wish we had had time to learn it—in fact, we have thought of putting in a few months with a blacksmith ourselves. He ought also to learn welding iron and steel, brazing, and tempering such things as the tines of a fork. Carpentering, too, is very useful ; what we learnt from

Everson, as the putting up a cow-shed, was invaluable. He should be able to cobble a little and mend his own clothes. Book-keeping is quite indispensable if you mean to run a farm. Gardening is also a good thing to know. Our outfit was just about complete. Some coarse cotton shirts, as they keep out the thistles and the barley-beards, would have been an advantage ; flannel shirts make you like a pincushion directly. A big fur cap, round and large enough to cover the ears, would also have been an advantage. Flannel shirts should be of very coarse material ; good flannel is useless. Some light strong breeches, as well as corduroys, are useful for the summer. It is well not to have many cloth clothes, and a light mackintosh is better than a heavy waterproof. The india-rubber baths, which we did not bring, would have been very useful.

CHAPTER VI.

February.—A short time ago we had a blizzard which lasted for four days. It did not blow very cold, but the snow drifted tremendously. One day the mail-train, which was due at 12.20, passed at 3 a.m. the next morning. Next day Mr. B—— and I went up the mountain. The roads were in grand condition, the snow being drifted eight or nine feet deep in some places. Coming down one steep slope the horses slipped, or, rather, sat down, and we all had a sort of toboggan slide for about a hundred and fifty yards. Fortunately the snow was deep enough to prevent our getting up any very great speed. Twice I had to jump out and hold up the cutter to prevent its upsetting. Soon we expect to go up there to haul lumber to the saw-mill.

Lately we have been drawing firewood from the bush. It is first sawn into lengths of four feet, and then split and piled on the sleigh crossways. It is terrifically hard work for the horses, as the loaded sleighs have to be drawn over trunks of trees, and through the under-bush. There were also numbers of holes, made by the tearing up of trees in the high wind. We turned one load clean over, and had to put it on again. With the other load we did very well till we reached a big hole—and then 'chuck' went the front bob of the sleigh into the hole, and weight and jerk together broke the centre of one of the side-beams. The wood was piled on again, and then in trying to draw out of the hole the horses drew clean away from the sleigh and bent the draw-bolt, which is quite an inch thick. We had to chain them to the sleigh after that, as we had no means of straightening the bolt. But after a bit we got away all right, though the horse's legs were awfully cut about by their sharp shoes when they plunged into the deep snow.

March.—The day before yesterday one of the yearling colts got upset into a manger in the stable, and, not being discovered, it remained there for some hours, on its back the whole time. When we found it, it was necessary to chop the manger down with an axe to get it out, and then it was utterly unable to move. We spent about two hours rubbing its back and legs, then we rolled it into a flat kind of sleigh, called a ' stone-boat,' and brought it down to a warmer stable. We gave it gruel and linseed-tea several times during the evening, and it seemed so much better at ten o'clock that we thought there was no need to sit with it ; but yesterday its head was awfully swollen, and it could not eat. In the evening we had to kill the poor beast, as inflammation of the bowels set in. That seldom lasts more than half an hour, so it was better to put it out of its pain.

To-day the 'Chinook' is blowing, and we were able to dress with our window wide open. Only three days ago the thermometer was down to 20° below zero.

Dick and I have started to teach ourselves book-keeping, as it would be little use to try to run a farm if we could not keep our books properly. We found it pretty stiff at first, but now we get on swimmingly. We spend about an hour and a half at it every evening.

March.—This morning Dick and I had half an hour's skating, but the ice was very poor. It is the first we have had this winter. Sleighing is nearly gone now, as the roads in some places are quite bare. Yesterday I drove a load of lumber to C——. We made a road for the occasion through fields covered with ice, and over ploughed fields as well, which were often bare. It is ticklish work to avoid the stumps and stones when driving over bare places.

Two days ago I started to walk up the mountain, to meet some cattle about seven miles from here. If they did not come, I was to go on and bring them back next day. They turned up all right, and then came the business of driving them home. They were completely tired out, as they had already come some eight miles; added to this, the roads were in a frightful state—two feet of soft snow in most places, and where that had gone, a foot of mud. I had a very lively time. The cattle tried to take every new road that we came to, and made a rush for every gate. However, by dint of a long stick and incessant yelling. I got them into a very obedient state. The 'boss' has just sacked the man who did all the cattle-feeding and milking, or, rather, the man has just sacked the 'boss,' so the milking has again devolved on me.

To-morrow we begin drawing ice from the lake. It is cut into blocks about two feet cube, and then about a ton and a half is put on to a sleigh. We pack it all in an ice-house, fill up the cracks with small slips, and then pour water to freeze it all solid; after this we cover with eighteen inches of sawdust. The ice will keep about fourteen months, perhaps more.

Dick and I are proceeding like a house on fire with the book-keeping. We can now do simple keeping, and can balance and close the ledger. Do you know, I have quite a reputation here as a doctor. Twice I have been asked to look at children, 'as you are something of a doctor.' One had the measles, and the other inflammation of the lungs. You would be astonished at the sudden

changes of temperature which we have here.
The climate is very changeable, much more so
than in the North-West, so far as I can learn.
Here are some temperatures taken at 7 a.m. :

February 21st ... -8°	March 1st ... 12°
„ 22nd.. -20°	„ 2nd... 34°
„ 23rd ... -8°	„ 3rd ... 16°
„ 24th ... -28°	„ 4th ... 6°
„ 25th ... 0°	„ 5th ... 18°
„ 26th ... 23°	„ 6th ... 22°
„ 27th ... -20°	„ 7th ... 34°
„ 28th ... 0°	„ 8th ... 20°

March.—I was sorry to hear the unsatisfac-
tory news which you gave of the X——s ; I
should have thought they would have succeeded
if anyone would.   But it is very hard to make
grain-farming pay, unless you have a very
good capital to start with, and, besides this,
they have had very bad corn seasons lately in
Manitoba.

Now about going North-West.   First I
must try and disabuse you of the notion that

the work there is harder than it is here. In this place the work begins at 6 a.m., sometimes at 4.30—on a small farm it begins regularly at 5. In both cases it continues till 8 or 9 at night. As all the time you are working in conjunction with other men, you have to work your best, for if you fall behind, it becomes twice as hard at once. In the North-West, work on a cattle-farm would begin about 5, and would not last so long, except on extraordinary occasions ; perhaps once or twice a month we should require to be in the saddle all night as well as all day. But the work would not require nearly so much strength, as it would be chiefly herding cattle. After the first trouble of getting used to spending so much time in the saddle, it would not fall so heavily on us. Of work in the North-West I only speak from what I have heard ; of the work here I have had experience. Still, if we found cow-boy life too hard we would try to get work on other farms—this would not be hard, I understand. As to living, it would be much the same as it is here.   Of course we should have to camp out a good deal at night, but that would be a blessing, and not a hardship.   If we go on to a ranche in the North-West, we could, in a year or two, save enough to start with, as the wages there are high.   When we have done this, we should take up a little land, two to three hundred acres, and keep bees, poultry, and a few cows—also we could grow fruit.   In addition to this we should keep a team, and for the first year or two one of us might hire out with the team by the day, whenever we had no work of our own for it.   He would earn $2 or $3 a day, and so would help the farm considerably.   This would require very little capital to start, and is one of the most paying branches of farming.   The two of us could take up three hundred acres of land, and by complying with the requirements of the Land Office, by cultivating a part of it, could, in three years' time, get complete possession of it. Then if we found we wanted capital we could sell part of it—say fifty acres—which, if you had worked pretty well, and had land well situated, would fetch from $500 to $1,000. You see, therefore, that time is a consideration to us. Everybody we meet advises us to go. We shall earn good wages there, as by that time we shall be competent book-keepers. Here the wages are miserably poor. People pay labourers as little as they can, and get as much as possible out of them for that little.

Though the 'boss' has said several times that it is best to stay here, he actually thought seriously at one time of giving up the farm here, and going North-West himself. We shall get on well with riding there, and after we have acquired some experience there of cattle, there will be no difficulty in getting 'passes' to British Columbia, if we should wish to try that. Another good reason for going is the climate.   Here, as the residents themselves confess, it is detestably changeable. By the way, we have both taken to wearing cholera belts, so that the weather, however suddenly it changes, cannot affect our insides.

We are going to speak to the 'boss' to-night about getting off in the beginning of May, and as to the chance of getting ' cattle-passes.' As we shall be unable to let you know what way we go in time for your answer to reach us, you had better send the £30 at once.   If everything goes as we hope, we shall not have need for anything like this sum; still, it is best to be on the safe side, and you may be sure that the money will not be spent unnecessarily. The short time which we have put in in this country has taught us to be economical.   A cheque will, I think, be the best way, though perhaps a draft is safer.

What you said about woollen underclothing is certainly right. Even on the hottest summer days, when from the nature of our work we have to wear cotton shirts, a thin vest is always advisable. You asked some questions about the way of living here. For breakfast we have meat and bread-and-butter, *ad lib.* The meat during the winter is beef, either fresh or salted. At dinner, meat, potatoes, sometimes cabbages, or beans and turnips, also puddings of different kinds. Occasionally soup takes the place of pudding. For tea there is meat again, fruit, and bread-and-butter. There is very little hardship about the living.

April.—The winter has really broken up here, I think, and the snow is disappearing fast. The days now are splendidly warm, as the sun is very strong ; but the nights, till last night, have still been pretty cold—about 22° F. of frost. All the roads are about six inches deep in mud and water. Lambs are quite plentiful now, and the birds are beginning to come back ; in fact, we can both feel

6

and hear the spring returning. We have been breaking in two three-year-old colts lately ; one has been in harness four times and has run away twice. The other day I rather astonished him. I wanted to take him down to the driving-horses' stable, so I caught and bridled him. I had quite a job to do it. Then, when he stood still for a minute, I jumped on his back. He had never experienced anything of the sort before, and did not know what on earth to do. For about half a minute he stood stock-still, and then started to go backwards, chiefly on his hind-legs. After doing this for a short time I got him to go forward in a sort of fashion, but it was mostly sideways. At last one of the men came up behind with a long stick, and gave him a couple of whacks, and off he went in fine style. Now he goes quite easily, though it is not safe to make him canter, or go beyond a slow trot, as he would probably try some tricks, and we don't want him to get into that way. I do not get on him now, as I'm a bit too heavy for him. The other colt has only been in harness once ; he has a pretty bad temper, and it would take very little to make him kick furiously ; also he is as obstinate as a mule. All this week Dick and I have been cleaning wheat to send to the flour-mill at C——. It is very slow sort of work ; one turns the crank of the fanning-mill, while the other keeps the hopper full ; when we get about fifty bushels cleaned, we bag it up, and start on another lot. Fifty bushels, or twenty-five bags, make one load for a sleigh, and a pretty heavy load, too, when the roads are bad. Drawing out manure from the stable-yards has commenced now, and we have done a good deal of it ; still, it is not half bad sort of work, after all, though, of course, there are other things which are preferable.

Mrs. B—— has recommended that we should get some mittens made here of factory yarn, which costs about sixty cents a pound, and have them faced with skeepskin ; she said she would get some of the people round here to knit them, for some of our old clothes —a good plan, I think. The ordinary Berlin-wool mittens cannot stand the rough wear, though they are very good and warm to wear when not at work. A pound of wool would make four pair.

The snow has not quite disappeared yet ; yesterday at noon the temperature was 68° F. in the shade, and at night it did not go below 52°. This very moment it is 72° in the shade. The thaw has been tremendously rapid, and on Friday, which is usually kept as a Sunday here, we were working all the afternoon, stopping ice at the water-gate of the dam, in order to let the water get away. The ice had broken into blocks weighing about half a ton. These kept striking against the planks so that we could not take them off; we had to stand on the blocks, which

were swaying and heaving in a fairly lively
way, and chop the corners off, so as to let the
water carry them over the edge of the planks.
The really lively part was getting off after
you had set them free and before they went
over. Here is a little sketch of the dam—

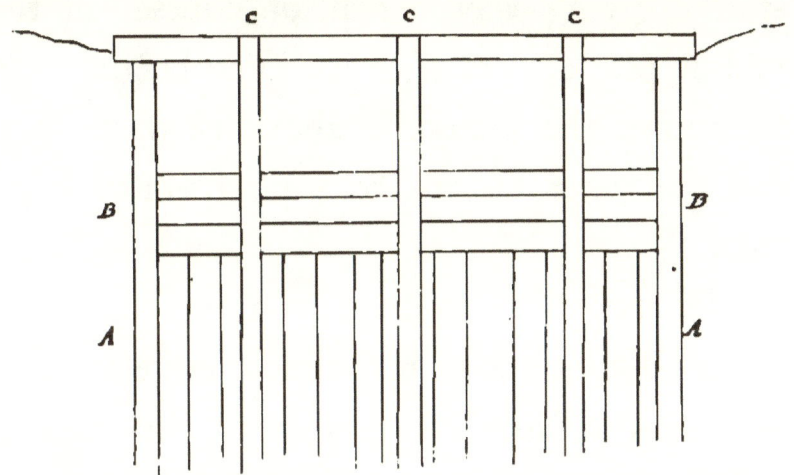

A, solid immovable woodwork ; height 12 to
14 feet. B, movable planks for letting the
water go over faster or slower, by taking
them off or putting them on. *c c c*, upright
studs against which the planks were held by
the force of the water. The ice jammed
against the top of B, so that the planks could

not be taken off. Blocks too large to go between *c c c* had to be stopped.   Last night the ice jammed again, and the water rose so high in consequence that it flowed over the top of the dam in several places further along. The dam itself was only saved by the centre stud *c* giving way, when, of course, all the middle planks went with it.   The height from the top of the planks is about 18 to 20 feet, and the water falls on to a platform of large logs.

We are going to send you two or three skins.   The mink-skin is almost large enough to make a muff.   You must be careful of it, as it is worth something ; I have been offered $3·50 (14 shillings) for it already.   I shot it by the dam four or five days ago. This morning we saw the first chipmunk we have seen since the winter began.   It is one that last summer used to sit on the edge of a roof just outside our window, and this morning it appeared in its old place and chattered away in a manner peculiar to the species. It evidently took a great interest in the dressing process, for it watched us intently the whole time.

Just as I was finishing this letter we had an alarm of skunk. A fearful odour suddenly began to come in at the open windows, and a cry of 'Skunk!' arose at once. Dick rushed upstairs and came down with a loaded gun; but we could not find the animal, for it had made off, but even out of doors it was not hard to tell that there had been one.

PART II.

EXPLORING BRITISH COLUMBIA.

CHAPTER VII.

A Change of Plans.—Our Journey to Victoria.—A Rough Voyage.—Our Destination at Last.

In their last letters the lads proposed the plan of going North-West, and gave some idea of the way in which they intended to work. A few days after this an offer was made to them by an uncle in British Columbia. Mr. Z—— and his wife, who had gone there with a view to settling, were at that time engaged in looking out for a suitable locality. His proposal was to this effect : that the lads should come and join him in exploring the island of Texada. If, as he was inclined to think, this island should prove a desirable place, he further proposed that they should join him in running a farm of the same description as the

one they thought of starting near Calgary.
The offer was accepted, and at the end of
April they started to join their uncle at Victoria. The next letter, which was written
from Victoria, describes their journey to that
place :

May.—As I have not much time, I will
describe our journey to this place by giving
an extract from my diary. I am afraid it
is not very full, but it is all I had time
for :

Tuesday, April 26*th.*—Rose at 7 a.m., had
breakfast, and finished packing. After dinner
we carried our baggage to the station, came
back and said good-bye to the B——s, and
then caught the train at 3.35 to B——. We
arrived here about 6 p.m., and went to the
house of a fellow we knew. At 12 p.m. we
caught the train for North Bay, which landed
us there at 8 next morning. We slept all

night on seats without any cushions, which were slightly uncomfortable.

Wednesday.—The train which was to meet us was seven hours late, owing to having a very heavy load of cars, so we went off to the Pacific Hotel and had a very good breakfast for 20 cents each. I don't think they got much change out of us. Then we strolled about the place, and inspected the engine works, which are very extensive. After some dinner we stayed in the reading-room till 3.30, and then went down to the station. We got on a car which was going with our train, but it was an hour before the train itself came in. When it did come, it shunted about till 6.30.

At last we made a start for the West. At first there was some very rocky country, and we passed through two small tunnels, the first I have seen in Canada. When we came to the first of these there was an awful uproar among the colonials — probably they had

never seen such a thing before. During the
night we managed to get to sleep, but woke
up at odd times, thinking it was breakfast-
time. Three times—at 11, 1, and 3—did I
wake up with this hope, only to find that it
was a horrid delusion.

Thursday.—We woke finally at 4 o'clock,
and spent the time till breakfast in looking
out of the window. The country now
abounds with small lakes, not less than one
every mile of the track. They were absolutely covered with wild-fowl. After breakfast alternately dozed and looked at the
scenery, which has become very rugged. In
the evening we arrived at Port Arthur. There
was just time to buy a loaf of bread, when we
started again.

Friday.—At 7 next morning we arrived
at Rat Portage. We got out here and were
driven in a large dray, at full gallop, to the
Queen's Hotel. Here we had breakfast. The
country has now become rather flatter, and is

more or less heavily wooded. Near Winnipeg itself it is almost absolutely level and void of trees. At last we found ourselves upon the 'Boundless Prairies.'

At 2 o'clock we reached Winnipeg. Here we found an immense crowd at the station. We got out, and rushed about to find the train for the West. We were only just in time to get seats, though the train did not start for another hour or more. It was awfully crowded, and for the first few stations many had to stand. The country was, if possible, more level than before, studded every now and then with farmhouses. One of these, about thirty miles from Winnipeg, was on fire.

Saturday.—We reached Brandon about 7 in the evening. Here the thermometer stood at 70° in the shade. The prairie here is rolling and hilly ; there are plenty of streams and pools which are covered with wild-fowl. Brandon is a very nice place, and is supposed to be the most prosperous town in Manitoba. The prairies, which have been a brown colour till now, have begun to get greener. There has been a scarcity of rain in these parts for a year or two.

All the prairie about here is strewed with buffalo-bones, many carloads of which are shipped to the sugar refineries. During the morning we saw some deer and, later, a caravan of waggons going over the plain. The plain is lined with old buffalo-trails leading to the deepest pools, which have water in summer. There is still a little snow to be seen among the recesses of the hills.

Our travelling is at an average rate of thirty miles an hour. In the train dining-car you can get a pretty good dinner for 75 cents —soup, salmon, lamb, four kinds of vegetables (including green peas), apple-tart, and dessert. The country through which we have passed during the latter part of to-day is covered with about an inch of snow—the reason is that we have run into a snowstorm. As we approached Medicine Hat the country became a good deal more varied and interesting ; in parts it was quite hilly. At Medicine Hat some Indians came and tried to sell polished buffalo-horns. Whether they were real or not I can't say—probably there were some of both. After this the country again became absolutely flat and desolate, apparently no settlements at all. Once we had to stop some time to allow a herd of cattle to get off the track.

About midnight we reached Calgary. Naturally we could not see much of it. Directly we stopped, crowds of people swarmed on to the cars to see who was there. I got on to the platform for a moment, and immediately a crowd of people poked their faces close to mine, and inspected me, so I got back again. We started again in about twenty minutes.

Sunday.—This morning we found ourselves

7

entering the Rockies. As we go on the scenery becomes splendid. On each side of us are great peaks covered with snow, and with great masses of pine-trees. Everywhere the snow is about three inches deep, and the weather is rather cold. The railway lies between two great ranges of hills thickly covered with pine forests. The sun is just now rising, and the snow-topped mountain peaks standing out against the deep-blue background of the sky look splendid as the light is thrown upon them. Occasionally we pass houses which are inhabited by men who have to look after the track. We breakfasted at Field.

About 1.30, after another halt, we passed over a wooden bridge two hundred feet high. We stopped once because of landslips, which had to be shovelled out of the track—the melting snow on the mountains makes the land very unstable. When we went uphill we had an engine behind to help shove. We passed two or three more bridges, about two hundred and fifty feet high, and then the highest on the C.P.R., three hundred feet high. It seemed awfully steep when we looked out of window, as there is no railing at the side. The line is now running along the edge of the cliff; on one side there is the sheer rock, and on the other a ravine about half a mile deep and two miles broad. There is a river winding along the bottom of it, and the banks are covered with pines.

The mountains here are about 10,000 feet above the sea-level, and 4,000 above the level of the plain. We have just now been passing under huge sheds, made to prevent the slidings of mountain snow carrying away the track. These sheds cover in the track altogether. The line here takes a most circuitous wind along by the foot of some tremendous peaks. About every five hundred yards we cross a bridge over some awful precipice.

Monday.—We woke at 5 a.m., and still found ourselves among the mountains, but they are not quite so high. Now and then there are some clear spots, and occasional Chinese settlements.

We reached New Westminster at 2.30, and caught the Victoria steamer. I was, fortunately, not ill. We reached Victoria at 9.30. The place swarms with Chinese with enormous pig-tails.

I can't write any more now. To-morrow we start early for Texada, being a party of five — Aunt K—— and Uncle W——, Herbert, myself, and a Greek sailor.

Texada Island.

May.—We started from Victoria on Friday (6th), and made about forty miles, getting into a small bay (Maple Bay) at 10.30 p.m. Next morning the wind was strong and squally, and we did not start till late. It was an awful job, the getting out of the bay, for we had to tack right across it several times ; and, when we did get into the open, a big squall came, and we had to let the mainsail fly, and then haul it down. The jib blew out of the bolt ropes directly after, and we rushed up the coast at the rate of ten miles an hour, under bare poles alone.

We got into Horse-Shoe Bay, Chemainus, at 3, wet through ; though we got warm at the last — the Greek, Dick, and myself taking the rowing boat, and towing the sloop down the bay to the wharf. We found an inn, where we dried our clothes and had tea, sleeping there on Sunday night as well.

On Monday we camped for the night on the north end of Thetis Island. We lit a fire and had coffee and biscuits, butter, hot potatoes, and fish. We cut some poles, and rigged up a big tarpaulin as a tent, and then put the boughs off the fir-poles on the ground, and spread the bedding on them, and the four of us slept on the top—the Greek always sleeps in the boat.

In the morning, after breakfast, we started

again.　The tides run very strong on this coast, and when we reached a place called Dod's Narrows (which is about seventy yards across), the tide running through at about ten knots, and the wind falling, we could not steer the boat one bit.　W—— had one of the long oars out, and pulled a bit on one side to keep us off the rocks, and went on pulling a few seconds too long, and we got caught in the whirlpool on the further side below the rapids, and were flung round twice, quite helpless ; and he, not taking his oar out of the water quick enough, got a dig in the ribs from the end of it.　I got hold of the other oar, and when we got clear of the whirlpool, we pulled away as hard as we could.　However, we could get no wind, and about a mile from the rapids we stopped to get some lunch. Before long we found that a back current was taking us back to the rapids at about three knots an hour, so we started to pull again. The wind came for a short time, and took us

on our way a bit, then it stopped, and we had
to tow into Nanaimo, where we had tea,
beds, and breakfast. All this time we have
been going north, along the east coast of
Vancouver Island, in among all the little
islands.

We started from Nanaimo in the morning,
with a good wind, and crossed to the mainland (ten miles) and coasted up to Normanby
Island, where we camped, sleeping on the
boat for fear of wolves. Next morning we
started again up the channel between Texada
Island and the mainland, but, having no wind,
only did ten miles, and then towed into an
inlet on the mainland, where we camped
The same thing happened next day, and, after
making ten miles, we towed into a bay at the
north-east part of Texada Island. Starting
again next morning, the wind failed us, and
we towed into this harbour, our destination.

W—— and K—— sleep in a tent, and
Dick and I in an old log-hut with no doors

or windows, and only one-third of the floor
down. Here the cooking is done with a
stove ; and it serves as general living-room.
W—— and K—— have been making
gigantic efforts to bake bread, and till the
last time made it rather like lead. The cooking is a terrible job to them every meal, and
it sounds very amusing to hear them blame
everything but the cook — the wood, the
stove, those who cut the wood, those who
light the fire, all get a share of the credit for
heavy bread, etc.

We have not done much exploring yet, but
at present the island seems to me all rocks
and stones, and one or two swamp meadows.
W——, however, seems much taken with it.
I went over to Comox (Vancouver Island) two
days ago ; the land there is first-rate, but
most of it is taken up. Harwood Island, too,
as far as we could see, would be a very nice
place. We may find good land on this island,
when we have explored it a bit more. Last

night the cove here was swarming with dog-fish, and they made a tremendous noise rush-ing about. I was lying on a log at the edge of the rocks, and pulled four out by their tails in about six minutes. We had a bathe, but the water was cold. There are a few big trees on this island ; we saw some yesterday which would have squared to four feet, one hundred feet from the ground, and were seven or eight in diameter at the base.

CHAPTER VIII.

The Island.—We go Exploring.—Chase After an Eagle.—A Savoury Dish.—Jubilee Day.

June.—At last we are seeing something of the backwoods, as we have come to an island the population of which, without ourselves, consists of exactly four. The country is extremely mountainous, with occasional swamps of a few acres in extent, and it is in the hope of finding a good-sized piece of this that we are staying here. At present we have only come across several small pieces and two or three small lakes which might be drained. There are very good markets for produce not far off, which would make dairying, and fruit-growing, poultry-keeping, etc., prosperous

work.   In the harbour there are heaps of fish,
and in the autumn there must be good hunt-
ing, as the place is alive with deer.   There
are also plenty of eagles—I know of eight
nests within a mile radius—ravens, crows,
water-fowl, and any number of humming-
birds.

Herbert and I sleep together in the old log
hut.   Our bed consists of a big tarpaulin on
the boards, then two grass mats, then a buffalo skin, fur upwards, lastly ourselves and
three blankets, our coats being the pillows.
We get up at 5.30, light a fire, get breakfast
ready and eat it, then go for an exploration,
getting back at 1 ; after lunch we explore
again, and get supper ready about 5.30 ; after
supper we read, or go for a walk ; bed about
9.30 or 10.

I am afraid my writing is not very good,
but I cannot do any better, as I am leaning
on one elbow and writing with the same arm
—we have no chairs or tables.   By-the-bye,

if you wish to improve your writing you must do it soon, for you are not likely to do it out here.

The weather now is beautiful, hardly any rain, as that nearly all comes in the autumn or winter. The last two or three days we have been exploring pretty hard. Yesterday we went to a lake, taking our fishing-tackle, and on reaching it I started to fish, while Herbert and W—— went round the lake. After a quarter of an hour I had a bite, and landed a lake-trout weighing half a pound. I was using paste then. Afterwards I tried artificial flies, and though the fish rose splendidly, I did not catch any, not being an adept in the art. These lake-trout are very game fish, and are splendid eating, having beautiful pink flesh.

To-day we went on another exploration, taking our lunch with us. After walking for two hours we arrived at a lake, and went round it, lunching on the further side. I fished during the time, having cut a splendid rod with my axe, and using this time cheese-paste, there being too many trees for flies. I used the cork of a bottle for a float, and soon had a fine bite. After playing a bit, as much as I was able without a winch, I landed a beautiful trout, weighing three-quarters of a pound. We did not stay much longer. so this was the only one I caught. These lakes have small, greenish mud-turtles in them, and a good many duck ; to-day we saw two or three broods in the reeds. After lunch we pushed on hard, going up some awful hills of pure rock covered with thick moss. After climbing nearly straight up for about four hours more, we reached about the middle of the island, where we could see the sea on both sides of us. We then turned back, taking a direct course to home as near as we could, with the help of a compass, which we have to use always on exploration here. We went fairly straight, striking our harbour about a mile and a quarter from the camp, which we reached about 6.20, feeling that we had had enough for one day.

When walking here we generally take a straight line by the compass, both going and coming. We can never go more than two miles an hour, as the country is very rough. Sometimes we come to a mass of fallen trees which have to be clambered over, sometimes to a deep ravine with a thick growth of young fir-trees which we have to push our way through, the ground all the time being rough and stony, full of holes and covered with rotten and fallen trees. Occasionally we chance on a green swamp, with from three to twelve inches of water in it, though many of them are nearly dry. These we go straight across, taking advantage of trees lying upon them. Sometimes in the bush we find gigantic trees blown down and lying in our direction, then we have a fair path for from 200 to 300 feet, but rather slippery, and ending in small chasms, from ten to thirty feet in depth. We have our boots nailed in order to be able to walk on these trees without slipping, as sometimes they have no bark, and on others it is wet, or very loose. We have bathed two or three times, but the beach is not nice, as it has quantities of barnacles on the stones, which make it decidedly unpleasant. There was a good deal of rain yesterday, though it soon cleared up again—we hardly felt it under the trees.

June.—A few days ago we went round the harbour, and just outside it, in the small boats, picking up drift wood for seats, tables, etc., for the camp. We got a boat-load, and arriving home at half-past one had lunch, and started to make benches. We sleep in a hut now above the main camp, about sixty or seventy feet higher up. To get to this we have to go up a very steep and winding path-way. I have seen nobody except our own party (not counting Indians) for nearly a month.

Yesterday Herbert and I went out shooting in the open boat along the shore, landing every now and then, as we were only rowing about ten yards from land, and stalking anything worth shooting. After rowing about twenty minutes, we spotted an eagle on a tree about a hundred yards in shore, so I landed Herbert with the rifle to stalk him, while I kept the gun in case he came my way. After about five minutes of anxious suspense, I heard first one, then another rifle-shot, and then a tremendous crashing, and saw Herbert coming towards me as hard as he could, carrying a great dead eagle, a splendid bird with a white head and tail, huge claws, and a beak that would make you pale to look at. It turned out that his first shot was successful in killing the bird ; his second wounded the mate, which managed to escape. We then continued our journey, and saw what we thought was the wounded eagle settle a little further on. I landed with my rifle, and made my way towards him, but he flew away and settled somewhere ahead, so we followed him up, and I landed again and saw him perched about seventy feet up, on a bare tree about sixty yards from the shore. I saw that I could not get up the cliff to the foot of the tree, so I fired at him from the beach, and saw him drop, as I thought. I scrambled up the cliff, and, after ten minutes' search, found a feather covered with blood; but that was all. At that moment I heard Herbert shout, and found that the eagle had contrived to drop into the sea, mortally wounded. He rowed after it, and managed to secure it after some trouble, as it was most ferocious, and lay on its back in the water, with just its head and claws appearing. He attacked it with an oar, which it promptly laid hold of with all its might, and was thus hauled into the boat. When I got in it made a savage onslaught on

my legs, but the corduroys were a good
armour against its claws. It turned out to
be the one Herbert had wounded. My shot
had gone through its leg and into its stomach,
thus nearly finishing it off. We had some
difficulty in killing it, as it was still very
lively.

This island positively swarms with eagles,
ravens, and crows. At the place where the
stream runs into the harbour, we found cart-
loads of dead herrings, most likely in consequence of a very high tide lately, when they
had been driven up the stream as far as the
tide went, and when that dropped had not
dared to go out, being left dry or killed by
the freshwater. The harbour here is always
full of herrings, sprats, etc., and there is a
great commotion when dog-fish come in,
hundreds leaping out of the water at a time,
and tremendous scrambles ensuing at the
surface. Every night before we go to bed
we have a systematic slaughter of mosquitoes ;

but they are not nearly so bad here as in Ontario. I have to use the greatest precision as regards my bed, for, if I alter my position an inch, I am nearly transfixed by a projecting edge of rock. If I can avoid this, I am very comfortable, as I get into a groove lined with moss.

Herbert and I have already made a kind of clothes-horse and an easy-chair to hold two out of the drift-wood.

June.—Last Monday we went for an exploration up to the north end of the island, passing by a spot where a forest fire had raged. It was positively awful walking, all the fallen trees being out of sight and covered with a thick undergrowth. We reached the sea on the other side, and, stopping to rest for ten minutes, started home again. About a mile and a half from home we saw a 'coon scuttling up a tree, so we went for it, and when we reached the foot of the tree, W—— went up after it.

When near the top he began cutting it off; half-way through he turned giddy and came down. I then went up, meaning to come to close quarters with the 'coon; when about two feet off him, he made a clear spring of thirty feet to the ground, were he was speedily put an end to. On Tuesday we skinned the 'coon, and got it ready for cooking, for as we had heard that the Yankees eat them, we determined to do so too. At supper we had roast 'coon, which was all very well if we had not known what it was, but, as we did, and had spent some hours skinning it, it was all we could do to do our duty to it. On Thursday an Indian came round in a canoe selling a deer he had shot; W—— bought half of it for fifty cents.

As we are on an island where there is only one settlement, and that consists of three houses, we have to go to Comox in Vancouver Island for all supplies. The sailing is not very good, as the wind is apt to get up quite suddenly.

The last time we crossed it was very bad indeed, and we came very near to being capsized. We were very nearly flat on the water, and two-thirds of the sail and mast were underneath.

There are some most beautiful humming-birds here—a sort of bronze all over. They have backs which shine like gold in the sunlight, bright crimson throats, and long curved beaks. Yesterday Herbert saw a panther, nothing very dangerous, but not a nice customer. As it was Jubilee Day, we hoisted the Union Jack on a tree just by our camp. In the evening we drank the Queen's health in punch.

CHAPTER IX.

The Way we Live Now.—More Exploring.—A Fine
View.—A Sudden Squall.—We Decide to Leave
the Island.

THE letter which begins this chapter was
written by the lady of the party encamped
upon Texada Island.

June.—Where we are now is a little nook in
a very pretty bay. It is a lovely place; but
when I say that there is scarcely a yard of
level ground, you will understand that it has
its drawbacks. We have, as I dare say you
know, a tent for W—— and myself, another
tent on the top of a little hill close by for the
boys, and a hut which serves for kitchen and
parlour. (Sailor John sleeps in the sloop.)

The ground our tent is pitched on is very uneven. I have to run up a hill to get to the washhand basin, and I invariably slide down backwards once, if not twice. There were rather deep holes where we made our bed, but W—— filled them up with pieces of rock ; then we put pine-boughs, then moss, after that a canvas blanket-cover, a buffalo robe, and finally blankets. It was really very comfortable, but lately W—— has made a really grand bedstead, as he thought it better to be further from the ground ; besides, it gives the spiders and beetles more trouble to get at us. The hut is a great convenience. We have our stove in it, with shelves for our stores. It has, it is true, no door and no windows, and three-fourths of the floor are gone ; but there is enough left for us. W—— and the boys have now made a table and four good benches, and we get on admirably well.

They, as you know, are busy exploring the island, and I sometimes go with them.

But exploring is not an easy thing in this country. No words, indeed, will adequately describe the places that have to be got over. Sometimes there are large masses of rock covering the ground, and there are smaller pieces everywhere. Then there are very thorny rose-bushes (with small, very red, sweet-smelling flowers, by the way) and blackberries, a very pretty shrub called 'sal-lal,' ferns, fir-trees, and any quantity of other bushes and trees. Then the ground is covered at intervals with fallen trees. Every few yards you have to get over one. Some you can step over, but most require a good climb. As for trying to go *round* them, that is out of the question, for many of them are over seventy yards long. Many of the large trees that are thus lying on the ground are quite rotten, and have a number of young fir-trees, some of them quite tall, growing all along their trunks. Sometimes they are useful for helping us to cross swamps. I am getting quite used to walking along them over hollows that are unpleasantly deep. Swamps there are in abundance, and lovely lakes, these latter full of trout. The boys have caught a few of these, but I look forward to their getting more, when they become more skilful. Deer are in plenty, but it is now the close time for them. However, we have had a taste of them, for two Siwashes (Indians) came over the other day in a canoe (the Siwashes seem to be allowed to kill them at any time), and W—— bought the hind-quarters of one for fifty cents and some tobacco. It was most delicious meat. Sometimes—I know you will like to know how we fare—we have cod from the bay. John cooks it cut up in pieces, with onions and tomatoes. It is eatable in this way, but not a very good fish after all. I am head-cook, though John, and indeed all, help. John has some Greek ways of dressing things which make them palatable. The bread, at first, was a great trial. I brought some bottles of yeast from Victoria, and made a dreadful mess of the first batch. Perhaps I used too little yeast; anyhow, the loaves would have done for ballast. Eventually they were sunk in the harbour, and I assure you that they went down like lead. At last I made some yeast for myself. Since then, and especially since I have been able to have some of that excellent Winnipeg flour, I have managed very well. We have hot rolls for breakfast. Imagine that! Sometimes John makes them, sometimes W —— or the boys. Then there is a supply of pilot-bread (or biscuits) to fall back on. One day last week they killed a 'coon, and when they had skinned it, thought that they would like it cooked for dinner. I remonstrated faintly, but was overruled. Indeed, I could not refuse when they offered to prepare it. And prepare it they did, and very nicely too, so that it looked just like a hare. At first they left the eyes in, but it looked so dreadful that I never could have basted it, especially as it had to sit with its head out of the oven-door. Even after the eyes were taken out it had a quite dreadful grin. Still, when it was cooked, it really looked very nice, and W—— and the boys seemed to eat it with great appetite. As for me, I got off with a very small piece. But, then, see the inconsistency of these creatures! Suddenly, when we were eating our pudding, W—— said, ' That 'coon was a trifle green ;' and one of the boys said, ' I am glad I ate it, and yet somehow I wish I hadn't,' and the other chimed in. So they all joined in vilifying the poor beast. I was not altogether surprised when I remembered that they had had their noses over it a good part of the afternoon. But 'coon is not an every-day luxury. For food generally, we have fish, tinned meats and soups, cheese, butter, syrup, cake, pie or pudding, and, of course, very admirable bread. The last thing at night we generally have some chocolate. Our great want is green vegetables, though the canned are tolerably good. Milk, of course, we have none, except the condensed.

As for clothes, the place is simple destruction to them. Cooking and walking through the bush would finish anything. W—— and the boys dress, if you can call it dressing, anyhow ; but W—— always puts on a collar for service on Sunday. I kept to collars as long as I had any clean. Now I wear embroidery. I have made vain endeavours to starch some collars myself, but, somehow, they won't come stiff. But I mean to try again.

We have some minor plagues. The mosquitoes are not much to complain of ; but the midges in the evening are a great pest. Not that they make any difference to me, but W—— and the boys complain of them loudly. Small flies, I am glad to say, do not trouble us, either in the house or out of doors. Other insects are innumerable—the ants are simply enormous, and there are bright beetles like those that are sometimes worn for ornament. There are crowds of mice, and I am always patching bags that they have eaten through. Yet they are so tame that one does not like to be hard upon them. There are numbers of butterflies, and some very pretty birds, some of which have a very nice song, but not so nice, I think, as our larks and blackbirds at home. There is one, W—— says, that reminds us of home with its note, something between a postman's knock and a policeman's rattle. The crows, of which there seem to be whole flocks, are *not* musical. When we first came they used to gather round our tents in the early morning, and waken us with their quarrelling. The boys thought of throwing boots at them, but were afraid they would carry them off. Besides the crows, there are eagles in abundance. The boys shot two fine specimens the other day. When I tell you that there are panthers in the island, I shall have about completed my list. One of the boys had a little adventure with one of them some short time ago. He went down into a swamp to cut a stick for a fishing-rod, and lo! in the bush which he had picked out there was a panther lying. He had nothing but his axe with him. The panther, happily, moved off; and so, when he had got his stick, did the boy. So no harm came of it; but he had a scare. So, my dear M——, this is 'the way we live now.'

July.—We are getting on a great deal better now. Yesterday we came across some really good land. We dug into it, and found there were ten feet of very good peat. This, with the quantities of dead fish which are thrown up, would make exceedingly good manure. Without much difficulty we could get tons of it to the harbour at low tide, and ship it away. Things look much brighter than they did a few days ago. You will be glad to hear that we are both remarkably well. The large amount of exercise which we take is making us grow like one o'clock, especially the sculling and rowing. You will guess what it is like when I tell you that the waistcoats, which were made much too large for me, will not now meet across my chest by some two inches. Also, it is almost out of the question to button the coats. The pilot-coats are now just a nice fit, and are, without exception, the most comfortable things for wear that we ever came across. You just put one on, and lie down anywhere, with something for a pillow, and you feel as if you were in a feather-bed for softness and warmth. We are both very brown, and I think that you would consider us very dangerous-looking ruffians if you saw us when we go exploring in the bush. Long boots, corduroys, a check shirt, and a felt tennis-hat, with the brim well pulled down, form our costume. Sometimes we carry a rifle or a hatchet. The long knives, too, add something of the ruffian to our appearance. I have not looked in a looking-glass for over a month now, and, what is more, have not the slightest wish to do so.

To-day we went out to follow the course of a certain stream, and fix the position of some swamps. We found about fifteen acres of swamp and bottom land, and a biggish lake. On the other side of this was a howling wilderness of rock and forest. We found another stream running into the lake, and followed it. After an hour's hard walking we found ourselves within five minutes' walk of the place from which we had started. The stream had wound about in the most extra-ordinary fashion. Once we saw a splendid buck within easy range. It stood still and looked at us. But, alas! we had not the rifle.

We also found that the beavers had been mending and raising an old dam within the last twenty-four hours. There were lots of footmarks, so there must be some about still. The Siwashes, however, have killed most of them. In a day or two we go further down the island. Here we hope to find larger stretches of good land.

July. — As you have been some time without a letter, I will give you a description of what we have been doing during the last few days. On Wednesday the three of us rowed about four miles down the island to find a new camping-ground. We went to a bay where there is a river running out. We hope to find some good land somewhere along the course of this. We found an old hut in very fair condition. The only drawback was a large hole burnt in the middle of it by the Siwashes. But this we can board over. We came across one or two deserted logging-camps, and shot a brace of grouse. On Thursday we rowed to a Siwash village, where there is a Roman Catholic mission. Most of the inhabitants were out fishing or shooting. The Padre was also away, so we started home again. We rowed considerably over twenty miles that day, and the sun was awfully hot. In first crossing the channel we sighted a huge whale. It gradually got nearer and nearer to us, and then disappeared. After a bit it suddenly came up about thirty yards to one side of us, making straight in our direction. W—— and I were rowing, and you bet we didn't stop to watch. We made the boat go pretty quick, and the whale passed just by our stern. Coming home we saw no less than seven whales in different parts of the channel—now while I am writing I can hear them blowing. On Saturday we went to camp by the river which we found on Thursday. We rigged up a tarpaulin for

K—— and W——, and Dick and I found a nice little hollow behind a tree under some bushes. First we spread a waterproof sheet : then folded our coats into pillows, and, with our guns and knives handy, lay down and pulled the blankets and another waterproof sheet over us. We were very comfortable indeed, as the sal-lal bushes on the top of which we were made a sort of spring-mattress. It was necessary to have our arms ready, as we were some five-and-twenty yards from the camp-fire, and the whole place was swarming with gray wolves. On Sunday we took a walk up the river. After going some way we came to a splendid fall. The river ran through a narrow gorge about thirty feet broad. The whole gorge was on a tremendous incline, and it was headed by the fall where the water came sheer down some twenty feet. We could feel the ground shake quite a quarter of a mile away, and a large cloud of mist and spray hung over the falls. We then climbed on to a hill which was near, and from there saw the grandest piece of scenery I have come upon since we passed the Selkirks. The river came from a large lake several miles long and one or two broad. All round it were steep hills covered with timber ; and in the background rose the Cascade Mountains, capped with snow. In the evening there was the most magnificent sunset that I have ever seen. It was really beyond description. I was looking over the smooth sea dotted all round with little islands, and lit up with a bright red light. Behind the sea rose up the mountain-range along the coast of Vancouver Island, while behind them again were the snow mountains, their white peaks shining with a brilliant flame-colour: the clouds just above the mountains were edged with the same hue, and the whole sky was reddened with the light. This lasted about half an hour, and then the whole sky changed to a wonderful steel gray, which was almost as beautiful, though quite different. You could not realize a quarter of its beauty from the best description. I only hope you will be able to see something similar soon, when you come out here. There is lots of fun in camping out here, and the scenery is very grand indeed—almost too grand and rugged, I think. For my part, I should like to see a little bit of the scenery you get— green fields and farmhouses—better than all the mountains in British Columbia. Before long, however, I hope we shall be doing something towards making part of the scenery a little less wild. Perhaps then the rest will become pleasanter by contrast.

July.—The day we posted our last letters to you we went to Comox in the sloop. The wind fell almost directly after we had started, so we had to pull the sloop by means of the two sweeps, a man at each. We pulled here twenty-two miles, and can feel it now in our left hands, which got rather cramped. Coming back next day the wind again fell in somewhat of the same way. We got out the sweeps; but after we had been pulling for two hours a regular storm got up suddenly, and the sea was running very high indeed in less than ten minutes from the time when it had been like glass. We were only just able to beat round the point ahead of us. If we had failed to do this, I don't know what would have happened. Once round that, we made good time down to the harbour. We have been doing a little prospecting lately for minerals, but have found nothing except a few small veins not worth troubling about. The place is all jumbled up by earthquakes and upheavals and things of that kind, so that it is almost impossible to find really large ledges or veins.

We shall not stay in this island much longer. There is not sufficient good land to make it worth our while to start a farm here. After all, I think we shall go back to our old plan, and make our way to Calgary. Of

course it is rather a disappointment not finding anything here, but still it is plain there is
nothing, and so we must make the best of
things.

PART III.

ALBERTA.

CHAPTER X.

Calgary.

August.—You will be somewhat surprised to
see the name at the head of this letter. We
have been here now about three days, and have
been looking out for work. This, I'm glad
to say, we have got ; it is on a horse-ranche
five miles from here. The pay is $15 each
a month and board. The arrangement is
only for a month, but we shall stay on longer
if we can agree with the man about wages.
$15 is very low; but as we saw no immediate
chance of better, we determined to take it.
The country round here looks very nice as
far as we have seen, but we cannot, of course,

judge yet. Perhaps you would like to hear
something of our journey here. We took
seven days to go from Comox to Victoria in
the sloop—the distance is about 140 miles.
Of these we had to pull at least 80, as we
had either no winds or head-winds. The
only fair wind we had was in Victoria Harbour,
a little too late for use. We left Victoria on
a Sunday at 2 a.m., reaching Vancouver at 9.
We had a bath and something to eat, and
then started to come up the Fraser River
Valley. The mosquitoes nearly crowded us
out of the cars. I never saw anything like
them. All the inhabitants wore nets over
their heads. We crossed over 1,200 bridges,
ranging from 5 feet high and a yard or two
across, to 300 feet high and 300 or 400 yards
long. In some places the mountains were
very smoky, though not nearly so bad as represented in reports. Certainly, though, there
have been very large fires about.

When at Comox we were offered $20

a month each, and board, on separate farms ; I was for taking it, but Dick didn't like it, and so we came here. I hope you like the eagle's wings. We are both in excellent health.

You would be amused to see us riding about on our Mexican saddles, which are, by the way, awfully clumsy and uncomfortable. They weigh 30 lb., and sometimes more. The ponies are the scrubbiest-looking animals I have ever seen ; yet they carry you wonderfully well over the roughest ground. The saddles have what is called a 'horse' in front, on which you sling your lasso, and anything else you wish to carry with you. The stirrups are large wooden affairs, with leather in front to keep bushes from catching your feet.

Our plans must depend on seeing land which we like. The money, I think, we can save, as the wages we can get will be from $20 (£5) to $40 (£10) a month, and board,

and we shall have very few expenses. It does
not seem much to start on, but we can get
320 acres of land for $20 (£5), in fees ; and
for living on it, 320 more for $1 per acre, to
be paid in three years (if we still want the
land). We ought to start soon, so as to get
land near the town. It costs very little to
live if you have cows and poultry, and one or
two small things of your own to help you
on ; and, if necessary, one could work out
part of the time with a team and earn $60
(£12) a month. By the way, a first-class
team and waggon would only cost £70 ; other
prices are equally low, so we could start a
good many small things, to be gradually increased.

Living here is of a somewhat simple nature;
in fact, pork, damper, and tea ; damper, pork,
and tea; and tea, damper, pork, are the
varieties in which we indulge. Occasionally,
however, bread is substituted for damper.
We get up now at 5.30. Dick milks, and

I look after two thorough-bred horses. At 6.30 we breakfast, and then draw hay off the prairies. Twice a week one of us rides round the fences to see that they are in good order. We hope soon to get on to a farm where cattle require to be herded, as that will give us good opportunities for inspecting the land round. The country seems to be a very fine one. It consists chiefly of great rolling hills with streams winding amongst them. The mosquitoes, however, are simply awful. Calgary is a very go-ahead town, and is growing at a tremendous pace.

September.—The son of our host here has told us of two good spots about forty miles from Calgary—that is, about a day and a half's journey by waggon. They are valleys bordering on streams, with plenty of timber at hand. There is plenty of natural hay, and a considerable amount of game. During the winter there is rather more snow than in Calgary, which is a decided advantage. This place—I speak now of the best of the two—is within easy reach of the projected railway from Calgary to Edmonton, which is to be commenced next year. To get a place nearer Calgary, besides being hard to do, would not be any greater advantage over a place forty miles off, as under that distance no good amount of timber can be found. If possible, we want to secure some land in the district I have spoken of, and to do this we must be quick, as considerable tracts of land are being taken up every year. We have just seen in a paper that a large party of Ontario farmers had started West from Winnipeg to spy out the land. If we cannot get this place, we shall have to go more than forty-five miles from Calgary, which means another day's journey ; and this would make a great difference.

Now, if we could borrow £200, we should next spring buy a team and waggon, and go for a week up country to fix on a location. If we found one that satisfied us, we should come back, send in our claim to the land office, work out for six months, and, in the succeeding fall, enter into possession finally. I think by that time we shall have had sufficient experience to start for ourselves, as we shall have been out here for two and a half years. By next fall we shall have about £100 of our own to add to the £200 which we should borrow. This would give us a great advantage in starting, as it will enable us to get things that will bring in a return the next year. We expect to be able to pay back the whole interest and capital in three years.

I think I have given all our plans and thoughts on this subject. Tell F—— that all round Calgary and the North-West generally there is splendid pike-fishing. Where we are now, we often change our salt pork for jack-steaks, and very good they are. We catch them with a spoon-bait from a canoe, and they give very fine sport; the general size is from 4 to 12 lb. I forgot to say that, though we should buy our provisions for the first six or nine months, yet we should doubtless be able to supply ourselves with fresh meat by means of our guns and rods.

T—— had better not come to us before we have been settled six months, as during that time we shall be roughing it a bit, and it would not do for him to do too much at first. Tell him to try and if possible learn how to thatch both houses and haystacks.

To-day Dick and I have just returned from Calgary. Dick rode down—looking a regular 'cow-boy'—on a small white 'cayeuse' or Indian pony, with a huge Mexican saddle, and stirrups with huge leather flaps to them. He wore his old gray coat, and a large gray felt 'sombrero' on his head; altogether he looked an awful ruffian. I drove down with Mr. G——, the owner of this ranche, as I am unable to walk, owing to an accidental stab which I gave myself with my large knife. I was trying a dodge for opening it with one hand, and it half-opened without my knowing it, and so I ran it about two inches into my right thigh. I was quite lame yesterday, but can get around all right to-day. The tourniquet braces came in very useful for bandaging, as we had not our regular medicine chest with us. We went into town chiefly to make use of a note of introduction to a Mr. M——. He was very kind indeed, and has taken all our luggage into his strong room till we get fixed for ourselves. We told him exactly how we stood, and he promised to write to a friend of his and get us places for the winter with a company which is working up at Reddeer River. He also said that we ought to start for ourselves at once if possible, and said we could do so very well indeed with £200 to £300. He very much approved of our ideas as to how and with what stock we should start. He was also very much taken with the notion of 'bee-keeping.' Very little is done here in that way, and so we could command almost any price we wished for honey. Fowls also he thought well of, and said they alone could feed us (eggs fetch 30 cents a dozen); he also said that when we had land fenced in we ought to keep sheep. He told us there would be difficulties and losses to contend with, but that if we made up our minds to succeed we were bound to do it. Further, he gave us a note to the land commissioner or agent, asking him to help us in the choice of land; and said that when we fixed on any section of country, we might come to him and he would show us the reports of the Government surveyors on that particular part. Then we ought to go on a few days' trip to see the land, and, if we liked it, take it up. If you object to the idea of borrowing, we can wait till we have saved enough to start; but the

result would be to place us further from Calgary, and we might not get such good land.
By the way, you will find, I think, somewhere
in my diary (which I sent off to-day), an
estimate we made when we first thought of
the plan. The prices named for horses and
cattle are high, but I think it best to get
first-rate stock at a high price, and not
second-rate beasts; the first *always* command
a certain value, and with the second you can
never be *sure* of getting more than half what
you paid for them.

Our first object, Mr. M—— said, 'is to
get land with good hay on it, good timber
near or on it, and with good water.' This
kind of land is getting harder to obtain every
year ; so, you see, we ought to hurry.

We left British Columbia, firstly, because
the climate is so hideously wet in winter and
spring ; and secondly, because what land is
not already taken up costs from £5 to £30
per acre to render it fit for cultivation. This

climate, as far as we can judge, is much superior.

A few days ago we went out duck-shooting in the slough—there is about two feet of water standing in it and any amount of mud. So we put on old clothes, and had a fairly good time. The duck were very wild, so we only managed to get five brace during the afternoon. Our guns have turned out very good ones, and are the admiration of all that see them. We could, if we liked, get £2 more than we gave for them, for people are always offering to buy them. But we shall stick to them, as good guns are not always easy to get out here.

CHAPTER XI.

Haying.—A Buck-Jumper.—We Buy a Team.—
Breaking them in.

September.—You will see by my heading that
we have left our last place. We went first to a
ranche on S—— Creek, which is twenty-five
miles south of Calgary, and were there for a
week haying. This was rather a tough job. To
begin with, we got a lift for twelve miles after
leaving Calgary ; but then we had to leave
our valise behind, and carry our bedding on
our backs and walk over eleven miles of rough
prairie. We got to the haying camp late in
the evening, to find that the high wind had
blown the tents down and had rendered it
almost impossible to cook ; so we had supper

off cold salt pork and sour bread which you could pull out in strings a yard long.

There was a severe frost every other night, and we had not enough bedding, and so could hardly get to sleep. By the way, if you get T—— any blankets to bring out, mind and get double ones—that is, two large ones sewn together. Single ones are worse than useless; a pair of double ones is the only thing to have. Dick and I, if we get permanent employment for the winter, are going to invest in a buffalo-robe, as a supplement to our bedding. A fellow who is leaving here has two to sell ; he only wants £4 for each, and the usual price is £6 to £7. After we left the haying camp we came to P—— Creek, which is half-way to Calgary, and are now living in a log hut with an English fellow who has been out here five years. He offered to let us make his 'shack' our headquarters till we should get fixed for the winter. It will save us an awful lot, as hotel charges here are gigantic. A day or two ago we went out shooting, and got three brace of snipe and a prairie chicken or two. They make grand eating, after living on salt pork and beans. One job we are trying to get is that of cutting rails. We should take a tent, stove, and some provisions, and go up into the bush for the winter, and spend the whole time cutting and piling rails, which could be drawn away by teams every day. We ought to be able to make from $1 to $2 a day each, besides our food. We may go up to Reddeer, fifty miles north of Calgary, to work for a ranching company there. We don't yet know what sort of work this last would be; but that does not matter much, as long as it carries us over the winter. This morning I tried to get on the only available horse, to go to a neighbouring ranche. It was a broncho, which three months ago was running wild in British Columbia; but my right leg being still a little stiff from the cut I got a fortnight ago,

I was not quick enough in getting properly seated before he started to jump and kick around—' bucking,' as it is called here. He threw me a complete somersault. I landed with my feet in the air, my shoulders reaching the ground first; it took my breath away completely for a time; and for two or three minutes, when I did breathe, I ' roared' like a broken-winded horse, only rather worse. However, I got H—— and Dick to hold him while I got seated. When I got to my destination, two and a half miles away, he was so much cooled off that I was able to bring our valise and 4 lb. of butter back, though I had to walk him all the way.

October.—I am glad you like the skins— they are hardly worth taking any trouble about; still, if we go north, we may be able to send you a few better ones. Yesterday I saw the rancher from Sheep Creek about cutting some rails, and he said ' he could not say if we could have the job yet,' which means he does not want us. Also, I saw the manager of some lumber mills here ; he said that he had promised all his places, but that if any men failed to turn up we might have the places. It would be $25 (£5) a month each and board, to last till the place froze up (one to three months). This morning I saw Mr M——, who is to write to a friend about getting us places on the ranche at Reddeer.

Calgary Fall Show is on now. If there is a chance, it would be a very good notion for Teddy to get into the way of thatching ; the great difficulty here is to make a good roof.

We are seriously thinking of buying a team of horses, waggon and harness at once, then getting a few provisions and starting out for a week or ten days looking at land. Our reason is this : we can hear of no work just yet—that is, for a fortnight or three weeks— and we want to be doing something mean-

while. If we could not get work for ourselves and team—and I think we could—
during the winter, a fellow here has promised
to keep the team all winter for the use of it.
Another reason is that horses are so much
cheaper now than in the spring; and, if we
can get two mares, we can get a return for
our money next spring, if we care to sell the
colts. If we do get work for them, it means
$1½ a day extra besides their keep. Again,
if we start for ourselves next year, it will
save us a lot of time; if we don't, we shall
get bigger wages and be more independent,
as we shall have private means of locomotion.
Probably long before you get this we shall
have cabled for some money; it would
take something between £40 and £50 to
do it.

We have lots of shooting now, and have
great feeds of wild duck, grouse (prairie-
chicken), and snipe; the last are awfully
good. When I was in Calgary last, I was

unable to get back for two nights ; the second I spent at a house three miles from here— very nice people indeed, English too. Dick shot a skunk just outside the shack, but its skin is not worth taking, as the hair is not tight in. Yesterday morning a lot of prairie-chicken came and woke us up by running about on the roof. H—— and I slipped out at once, but they flew before we could see them; however, we each got one as they went. There are seven or eight hanging in the cellar now. We go to Calgary on Monday to see about the team.

P.S.—We have just cabled for £40. I believe we have something like this amount still of our own. There is a team going which we cannot let slip. We are now going into Calgary to buy it—waggon, harness, and all. After that we shall start for a week's exploring.

October.—I am sorry not to have written to

you before ; but somehow a wandering sort of life does not seem conducive to keeping up a correspondence. Next year, if we have a place of our own, you may expect more letters. I hope you and A—— will come out and see us as soon as you can. I can promise you lots of sport—wild duck, prairie-chicken, snipe, deer, bear (black, grisly, and cinnamon), wolves (gray, timber, and prairie), also trout and pike fishing. If we take up land on little Reddeer River, all on the estate, except the grislies and cinnamon, and they will be within a few miles, and with them mountain lions—a kind of puma. We are feasting now every day on duck, chicken, or snipe, which we can shoot sometimes without going ten yards from the house. The snipe are the best eating we have had for a very long time.

I have just been trying a dodge for washing flannel things with ammonia. I think it will answer. The trial I gave it was very hard, as the things were exceptionally dirty.

This winter, in all probability, we shall stay where we are now, except when we get work at any distance off. If we are not able to get work for the winter for wages, we shall stay here, working with our team for board and lodging, and that of the team also. The work will consist of hauling logs to build stations from the bush to here, and also in hauling hay to Calgary for sale.

At present we are engaged in breaking in our team. We get an occasional job for a few days, helping with the harvesting, etc. We were very grateful for the draft. We received it (or rather the bank did) the day after we cabled, and, owing to its coming so quickly we were enabled to buy a splendid team of bay mares, before they were shipped with a lot of other horses to Ontario. We have also bought a waggon and a set of double harness with the money we saved this summer by our work. So we shall in future have a team and waggon, and we shall have a four times better chance of getting work this winter than we have had before.

We gave £40 for the team. It consists of two bay mares, one dark and the other light ; one is three years old, and the other four. They do not stand very high, but they are what is called ' low-heavies,' that is, with short legs and heavy bodies, very clean cut and neat, and not by any means what would be called bulky. They will in another year's time or so, when they are full-grown, be very strong. Everybody who has seen them has admired them, and when they are thoroughly broken in they will be worth from £50 to £60. We are going to call them ' Belle ' and ' Vi.'

It was rather a big business breaking them in, as they were awfully wild. Three days ago we started on the work, and this is what we did : first of all we separated a small bunch of horses from the main herd which was running free on the ranche ; this bunch we drove into a corral or enclosure. We then drove out, one by one, all the horses except the two we wanted ; then we fastened up the corral and began work. We first proceeded to lasso one of them. When this was done, the three of us held on to the other end and pulled with all our strength—the horse in the meantime rushing madly about the corral, rearing and jumping, striking with its front feet and lashing out behind. After about ten minutes, a difference became apparent. It had been lassoed with a slip noose, so it began to gasp and roar, and as the noose became tighter round its 'wind-pipe,' to stagger and reel, and finally fell over, its tongue hanging at full length from its mouth, perfectly black and dripping with blood. It, however, regained its feet again by a terrific struggle, but only to fall a second time. Then two of us sat on its head, and another tied its four feet together. We then put a strong rope halter on, and took the noose from off its neck. After a few minutes it began to revive, and tried to get on its feet. The end of the halter was next tied to the horn of the saddle, its feet were untied, and one of us pulled it round the corral by main force.

After a while we were able to hold the halter by hand, and slowly approach it, tickle its ears, and pat its neck. All this was done with the greatest caution, as the least quick movement would have terrified it. After a rest, one of us would hold the halter while another went at a respectful distance and drove the horse with a whip. Every time it flung itself about, a jerk of the halter would tend to convince it that it was no longer its own master.

When a few hours of this sort of thing had passed it became comparatively tame ; though when first tied up to the wall of a stable, it flung itself against the wall till huge bruises were raised over its eyes, and on any prominent parts of its head.

We drove them about eight miles, and put them into another corral for the night, and gave them hay. The next morning we had to throw it again, repeating the choking process, in order to replace a broken rope on its halter. For about three hours we led it with a halter, one going behind as before, till it would allow itself to be led without anyone driving it. The other horse was treated exactly in the same way, and both are now fairly submissive. Yesterday we put the harness on them for the first time, as all we had done so far was merely halter-breaking, a very small fragment of our labours.

We started off to fetch them after breakfast. When we got there we led them round a bit and took them to water, and then started home, each leading a horse. About half-way home we changed our mode of progression, and I went ahead, holding a rope with each hand, Herbert going behind and driving them. After about ten minutes they took it into their heads to get frightened, and both bolted off at full speed. I hung on for about forty yards, and then had to let go, as I had absolutely no check on them, only holding each with one hand ; the rope, pulling through my hand, blistered and rubbed the skin off all my fingers. After about fifteen minutes we cornered them up against a fence and managed to get hold of the long ropes attached to their halters, and then resumed our way home, arriving in about half an hour. We then tied them up to posts ; at first they pulled back and flung themselves about a bit, but soon got used to it. We next slowly put the harness on, during which they stood unusually quiet. After leading them round, separate, with the harness on, we tried to hitch them together, and then we had a great commotion. They twisted all about, and, finally, one threw itself, breaking its bridle to pieces. I sat on its head while Herbert separated it from the other. Then a fellow we knew arrived with a horse he had just bought, and which had been worked before. So we hitched them together, not till after a tremendous struggle, as his horse, although it had been worked, was much wilder than ours. However, after a regular fight, during which it struck out with its fore-feet at a tremendous rate, giving me two whacks, one on the leg and another on the ribs, but doing no damage, we hitched them to an empty waggon and drove around. They both went fairly quietly, one of us holding the reins and another holding the halter-rope.

In the afternoon our mail was brought to us from Calgary. I don't think there is any chance of our going back to British Columbia, as we are very much pleased with Calgary. To be sure, butter is 35 cents a pound, but for us that will be a greater advantage than drawback. For the last month we have had beautiful harvest-weather, not a drop of rain. We live regally, sometimes having snipe, or teal, or cold duck for breakfast; roast duck or grouse for dinner, and sundry wonderful puddings of our own manufacture. We have now a regular supply of wild-duck, as we shot five brace two days ago; they are in the cellar, hanging. We each consume half a duck at a meal, sometimes a whole one.

This morning we fetched a load of hay from the stacks, the colt going very well. After fetching the hay, we let the horses feed for half an hour, and then put the other colt in the waggon for the first time; she ran at full gallop for about two hundred yards and then quieted down, and we fetched a load of fence-rails and posts. Herbert and G—— then drove to a place two miles off to see some logs, etc., and I stayed behind and put up a small corral to put hay in, so as to keep stray animals from eating it. After two hours they came back—the colt quite tamed down. To-morrow we shall drive the two new colts into Calgary, when I shall post this letter.

October.—The team is really a splendid one. Both mares are in very good condition, and well matched. They pull tremendously. We had one of them out the other day, getting a load of logs for building, and when the waggon got into a mud-hole she pulled steadily, and so strongly that the old horse in with her could not hold his own, and was pulled back against the load—and then the hooks came off the whiffle-trees, and she nearly turned a somersault. We fixed up again, and she pulled almost the whole load out by herself.

We have not worked the other one since we drove them to Calgary ; she got hot then, and going through a creek gave her a chill, resulting in a slight attack of water-farcy, her hind leg swelling up to twice its right size. She was very quiet while we bathed it, as soon as she found that it relieved her. It is nearly right now, and she is feeling in such good spirits that this morning she tried to have some fun with Dick, and got on her hind legs to pat him with her fore-feet—somehow he didn't see the joke.

We have been building a log stable, and have got it about half done ; it will take about fifty logs to build it. I shall be glad when it is done, as it is rather hard on the horses, having to stand out in the cold with no shelter. We are not getting wages now, but I don't think our time is wasted, as we get our own and horses' feed, and we are breaking them as well as learning log-building ; when the team is fairly broken we shall have a very fair chance of getting work at any rate for most of the winter.

We don't intend to regularly cultivate our ground in the way of raising crops for sale ; we should only plough and sow enough oats to feed our work-horses, poultry, and pigs—

twenty to thirty acres would more than cover it.   Our chief interest would be dairying and poultry, as there is a good sale for butter and eggs, etc., in Calgary.   I don't think working-out here would give us enough experience to pay for not having land of our own, as all that people do here is to run cattle out on the prairie, put up hay for food, and grow oats.   I think we can learn better by treating our cattle according to good books, than by following the methods used here by the usual run of farmers, which are reckless to an extreme, and by which they lose great quantities of stock, and render their horses almost unmanageable.   Our team, which we have only handled for about ten days, is now a good deal gentler than the majority of old teams round here.

As to good land, there is not any unoccupied nearer than twenty-five miles from Calgary.   We want to get land which we can stick to ' for ever and ever.'   I don't see much good in getting your land into good shape, and then selling it. We don't look upon it as an investment, but rather as a means of getting a permanent and independent livelihood, and perhaps something more. This country will be just the place for T——, as it is a sure cure for asthma

CHAPTER XII.

A Fight with a Prairie Fire.—The Team turns out
Well. — The Winter Here. — Sport During the
Winter.

November.—On Sunday week (October 30th)
we had a great fight with a prairie fire. I had
driven into Calgary the day before. On Sunday
morning I saw the fire, and made out that
it was about seventeen miles off, and not far
from home. I started at once, and driving
back as fast as I could, got here at 12.30.
Dick and H—— were just setting off.
We changed horses, had something to eat,
and started. The fire was then about a
mile away, and we reached the place at
1.15. About twenty men were already

there. We set to work beating with wet
sacks, and kept this up till 10 p.m., when
a waggon came along with a supply of food
and a raw hide. The food was very welcome
—we had had nothing, you will remember,
since mid-day—the hide was hitched with
long ropes to two saddle-horses, and started,
one horse on each side of the line of fire,
the ropes being about twenty yards long,
so that the animals were out of the reach
of the flames. We had put a sack of earth
on the hide to weigh it down, and there
were long ropes at the side with men holding them. This was to guide it. The rest
of the fellows at work went behind with
their sacks to put out any spots of fire
left by the hide. Dick and I were among
these, and very fast we had to run most of
the time, for the horses were terribly scared
by the flames, and went at a great pace. We
had to keep up with them as well as we could,
for a spot of fire, if left for a minute, would

have spread and spoilt all the work of the hide. This we kept up till 4.30 a.m., with not more than five minutes' rest now and then, when we had to stop and wet the hide. Altogether, we went rather over thirty miles, going round the fire, and leaving off about five miles from home. By that time every one was dead-beat, the horses as much as the men. There were two teams and thirteen saddle-horses at work ; and those that had dragged the hide, in one little *coulée* (or valley) where the flames were ten or twelve feet high, were singed all over. When we got across, after the hottest three minutes I ever had or wish to have, every one's clothes were on fire. Dick had four large holes burnt in his breeches, and one side of my shirt was burnt off. The fire destroyed a few stacks, but did no serious damage. What would have happened had it been left, no one can tell. Such a job I hope never to see again. In the little *coulée* I spoke of, it was like a furnace. Every now and then the wind would come in a gust, and then the fire would travel faster than a horse could go. We got it out just in time, for when we had just finished the wind began to blow very strongly, and a small piece which we had not put out got up steam and rushed away east at a fearful pace. It reached Bow River (which was six miles off) in less than twenty minutes, and burnt a streak as clear as if a road had been made.

There was another fire burning on the other side of the Bow River. This was not put out till a slight fall of snow came, and finally settled it.

Yesterday I drove into Calgary in a 'go cart,' a sort of diminutive dog-cart. The horse, a 'broncho,' had never been driven single before, so I expected rather a lively time, especially as the cart was a borrowed one, and I had been warned not to drive fast over rough places for fear of its coming to grief. Directly the broncho's head was loosed, off he went as hard as he could tear over the rough prairie. I thought something would break every moment, but wonderful to say it held together. We are very much pleased with our team—they are real good pullers. The other day we went to fetch logs from the bush. We got four long green logs, awfully heavy. They are quite twenty-four feet long. Also, we had a shorter one measuring about eighteen feet. As the waggon was coupled too short, the weight was wholly thrown on the hind wheels, over which the logs were just balancing. Well, after we left the bush we came to a swamp, and of course the hind wheels sank in up to the hubs, and the waggon stopped. We rested the mares about two minutes, and then set off again. They pulled till I thought the harness would go, and the waggon slowly moved out of the swamp. This was pretty good, considering that they had brought the load about nine miles already. Last night we had rather a misfortune. Something got into the stable and scared the horses so much that one of the mares slipped her colt. It is a great pity, as next spring it would have been worth $30 or $40.

Dick, you will be pleased to hear, is bread-maker for the establishment. At this very moment he is making the dough up into loaves for baking. We are both first-rate cooks now, and can get up an awfully good feed out of bacon, beans, and flour, with a little grease. You would not know what was in the stuff, and would only think how good it was.

By the way, judging from your last letter, you seem to have rather an exaggerated idea of the winter here. Seven months long you call it, I think. We are now in the middle of November, and don't expect winter till after Christmas, though of course it may come any day. But if it came at once it could not last longer than four months: probably it will only last for two. Ploughing always begins here in March, when the frost is well out of the ground. We do, of course, have cold snaps here, and when it is cold it is cold, and no mistake.

November.—At last we have got a touch of winter. There is snow on the ground two inches thick, and that is as much as they ever have here; and last night the thermometer went down to 18° below zero. All yesterday it kept at about 5° below. Our cat was a little uncertain as to where she should locate herself. The oven-door happened to be open, and as she sometimes sleeps there, after sniffing around she got in. But before ten seconds were gone, she came out again in a pretty big hurry. The oven was a little warm even for 5° below zero. Next she got on to the dresser, which is close to the stove, and tried first with one paw and then the other to see if the stove-top was too hot. Apparently it was. Finally, however, she settled down on the plate in front of the stove, and remained there for the rest of the day, barring meal-times. This snap of cold has found us a little unprepared. We have been adding a new room on to the hut, and putting the logs on the roof has shaken down some of the plaster. The wind gets in quite a bit. However, we hope to have everything done in a week's time. To-day I have been nailing down the floor. While doing this I was interrupted by 'Vi' knocking with her foot against the water-tub to let us know she wanted something to drink. I suppose I had to get up and go out to her. They— 'Belle' and 'Vi'—are wonderfully quiet and affectionate now. Yesterday they stood quite still while I was picking the snow and ice off their feet and fetlocks. That means something, I can tell you, for the ice gets frozen on to the hair in large lumps, and takes some pulling before it will come off.

November.—You said in your last letter that you thought our method of taming horses was a bit cruel. Well, I guess it can't be helped. You see when we get them they are quite wild. There are other ways, of course, but they are far worse than the one we employed. There is plenty of water here in the winter, and plenty of sport, too. Snipe in any quantity. They are just like the English bird, and are brutes to hit, as they clear off at a terrible lick before you can get a sight of them. But they are awfully good eating. Also we have deer, wild cats, gray wolf, and last, but not least, 'the mountain lion.' They —the mountain lions—don't often come down our way. Now and then they make a raid on farms or ranches, anything in the way of sheep, calves or colts being very acceptable to them. They will not, however, attack a man unless provoked or driven into a corner. In the Rockies and in British Columbia there are plenty of them. The only objection to the shooting here is that you have to wade about in a huge marsh with the water up to your waist. This takes something off the pleasure, though you don't think so much about it if you are shooting for your larder. We are very comfortable here now, and like the life very much —it is healthy, and not too slow. Also there is money to be made if you stick at it, and don't get into the habit of going into the town too much. People seem to find it much harder out here to keep hold of money than to make it. As far as we can see, the best way to do that is to keep out of Calgary as much as is possible.

December.—I suppose this letter will reach you about Christmas-time ; so please give our love and best wishes all round. I wish we were at home to help with the provisions, as I guess you will miss us a bit in this respect ; but I know that the others will do their best to make up for us. The weather here has become pretty cold now. Our team, I'm sorry to say, are looking rather thin. We cannot get any oats for them, and hay alone is not good to work on. In a few days, however, there will be oats in plenty. To-morrow we take them to the blacksmith. I expect we shall have a fine time, as they will be terribly frightened. H——'s team will be worse than ours. One of his horses is, we think, really crazy ; no matter how kind or gentle you are to him, he will take the first opportunity to kick or strike you. A few days ago he nearly caught me ; but I was a bit too quick for him, and jumped into the manger just as his heels went whack against the logs.

CHAPTER XIII.

December.—We are having a regular North-West winter— -16° sometimes, and then 2° or 3° above freezing. Several days ago we watched the thermometer. In the morning, at 8 a.m., it stood at 16° F. ; two hours afterwards it went down to -3°. We then started to the bush ; when nearly there, I remarked to H—— on a peculiarity in the atmosphere ahead of us. It looked just as it does when you see the heat rising out of the ground on a hot day. Half a minute afterwards, down came a ' chinook ' on us, feeling quite hot compared with the cold wind before. Herbert, who was about 100 yards behind, heard my yell, but did not feel the wind till about two minutes afterwards, as it was travelling slowly, though, indeed, it increased to a gale in about an hour's time. We were not sorry to get it, as we have had an unprecedentedly early and long spell of cold weather. As we were going to the wood, we shot a partridge and a wood-grouse, also a 'whisky-John,' in winter plumage— the latter has a body as big as a robin, but larger limbs and tail.

I suppose, when this letter reaches you, you will be recovering slowly from the effects of Christmas dissipations. We, I'm afraid, shall not have much to recover from. Our Christmas-feed will probably consist of salt pork, boiled beans, and a jam or treacle tart with bread. Possibly we may manage to shoot a chicken or two; but they are getting awfully wild now and very hard to kill, owing to their enormously thick plumage. The 'chinook' that I spoke of has brought splendidly fine weather; while I am writing, though, it is freezing hard outside, as the wind has shifted into a more northerly quarter.

Two days ago we saddled 'Belle' and 'Vi' for the first time. 'Belle' bucked a little, over a waggon standing near, but was soon quiet again ; 'Vi,' however, put her feet, head and tail together in real earnest ; but she slipped and rolled over, frightening herself so much that she became quite subdued. We do not intend to use them as saddle-horses at all, but think it as well that they should be broken to it, in case it might be necessary.

M—— has just told me of a good place, ten or twelve miles out of Calgary, and we are going out to see it the first chance we get. If it is as good as M—— says, we ought to make quite as much as $500 a year out of putting up hay and selling it during the winter in Calgary. What we have to find out is, if there is good water in the place and timber near at hand. We shall have no difficulty in borrowing, as it would be as safe an investment as any out here. However, if there is any difficulty at all about it, I guess we can make a start without it next year if we rustle* hard enough. What is in favour of borrowing, though, is, that if a man starts with a little capital in this country he can go ahead three times as fast as one who has to rustle his start.

(Through the extreme kindness of a relative, the sum of £200 was presented to the two boys in order to assist them in starting for themselves. The news reached them on Christmas-eve.)

December.—We have written to X——. The news of his kindness in starting us free is the best possible Christmas gift you could have sent us. You can't think what a lot of anxiety it has taken from us. This gives us the sure chance of getting really good land,

* Work.

and makes us independent to a great extent of outside work.

The winter is getting on most satisfactorily. To-day the temperature was above freezing ; and there was a clear sky and plenty of sunshine. We shall stay in this locality now, and take land north of Calgary. Though all the land, for some seventy or eighty miles, has been taken to the south of Calgary, very little of that to the north has been touched. The reason is the difficulty of crossing the Bow River when bringing stock or produce to Calgary. This winter, however, a bridge is being built, and will be opened in a few weeks. Then, of course, there will be a rush for the best land, and we, being on the spot, will get a pull over the rest, I guess. We shall devote ourselves chiefly to horse-breeding at present. In time we shall get to selling grain and hay. Horse-breeding, however, strikes us as the thing to pay most, both now and in the future. Garden-fruit we shall have, of course ; but this is rather uncertain, owing to the small fall of snow here ; indeed, all kinds of crops here are rather uncertain, owing to the summer frosts. We are fairly well satisfied with the winter. There have been some pretty cold snaps—27° below zero was the worst ; but mild weather has been decidedly in the preponderance. In this country horses are turned out during the winters, just like cattle, and after the hardest winters have appeared robust, and even fat— little colts and all. Horse-breeding will not be such a risky business as it may seem. We have not had very much experience, it is true, but ever since we have been out here we have had more or less to do with them. Again, in this climate they are subject to very few diseases. We shall also keep a few cows and poultry. Our work will be something of this sort—herding horses morning and evening, branding them in the spring and fall, putting up hay for the riding and working horses during the winter, harvesting a crop of oats for our own use, putting up fences and stables. In addition to this, after three years' time, there would be buying and selling to be done, and shipping the animals off to Ontario or Manitoba, which are the chief markets. Of course we shall have to work pretty hard at first, putting up our log-hut, and some corrals, etc.; but we shall not mind that. Why doesn't M—— come out? If the idea that he will be of no use prevents him, let him forthwith dispel it from his mind. We would soon teach him what real work was, and make him think himself the hardest-worked brute in creation. At first, of course, we would let him off lightly as a greenhorn and a tenderfoot.

January, 1888.—We have been having a week of real winter. It would not have mattered if we had been ready for it. But the 'shack' is not properly plastered, there is no hay for the horses, as

the stacks are a mile and a quarter off, and
the supply of firewood and food is rather low.
The spirit in the thermometer has not been
within shouting-range of zero since Monday
week, excepting on one day, and then we all
rushed off to the bush ten miles away to get
more firewood. The snow is so deep now that
horses can hardly draw a waggon, and sleighs
are rare round here. Yesterday we borrowed
a sort of sleigh known as a jumper : it is very
low, and you sit just behind your team's heels.
Well, we started in this thing to Calgary, to
get some food. When we were three miles
on the way we had to stop and get thawed
out at a house, as the snow thrown up by the
horses' hoofs had frozen on our faces and
made it impossible to see. Finally we had
to turn round and come home. Then I
saddled a horse and rode over to a neighbour's and borrowed enough food to keep us
going till we can get some from Calgary. I
forgot to say that just as we got home the

pole came out of the jumper and the team went on, leaving us sprawling in the snow.

Tell cook that I've got a new dodge for bread-making instead of yeast. I think it is the same plan as that used in Palestine by the old Jews. The last time dough was made for bread I took a small piece of it and put it aside to get sour ; to-day, in making bread, I am using this sour piece of dough instead of yeast, for we have none of that left. The bread is not made yet, but is doing very well so far.

January.—I suppose that Christmas gaieties have not allowed you much time for writing ; at least, that is the way we account for absence of mail last Thursday. Dick and I walked three miles to the post-office and back again through snow which was knee-deep. When we got there, the only thing for us was a small circular from some book-seller in Calgary. We felt like going on to interview him at first, but afterwards thought better of it.

The day before yesterday we went with our team to get firewood, and had an awful time of it coming home. The snow was drifted three or four feet in lots of places, and very often the horses were up to their bodies in snow ; even where there were no drifts the trail was awfully heavy. We had ten miles of this, and, in order to lighten the horses' work, walked all the way back and most of the way there ; and this in a deep snow, with a crust not quite hard enough to bear your weight, and yet which held your feet at every step. We had got nearly home —half-way up the last hill—when the horses gave out, and tried to make little rushes to get on, not pulling steadily together. For a long time we had to stop, and let them get their strength again. Certainly they had done splendidly.

There is some talk of Dick and myself

going to the bush to camp out and cut rails
for two or three weeks. It seems a tempting
prospect, living in a tent with the thermometer often going down to -20° and -30° F.
However, a tent is very easily warmed, only
it gets very cold when the stove is out. Still,
if we go, we shall have lots of bedding. I
will tell you how much, to see if you think
it enough. First, a tick filled with hay; on
top of this one half of a double blanket,
then ourselves, then the second half of the
double blanket, and on top the two big white
blankets and the two blue ones we brought
out with us; then the two heavy ulsters, the
two waterproof sheets, the two white waterproofs and the pea-jackets; indeed, a man
needs a steam-crane to lift the bedclothes in
order to get up; but once in, you do not
find it a bit too much. The waterproofs go
half under and half over the bed, and keep
draughts from getting between the blankets.

You talk about fancy-dress balls and dinners,

etc., and then say the Christmas has not been so gay as usual. Why, to us poor devils, living in daily fear of losing some portion of our flesh from frostbite, with one long round of bacon and beans, it sounds like a paradise! We are considered quite 'old stagers' here, as people know we have been both in Ontario and British Columbia, and don't know quite how long either ; so we can talk of greenhorns.

CHAPTER XIV.

A Blizzard.—Out in the Bush.—Another Team.—Driving Downhill.—We take up Land.—Preparing it for Habitation.—We all Try to get Drowned.

February.—You must excuse the long interval between this letter and our last, as we have been camping out in the bush for seventeen days, cutting posts and rails. By the way, you need be under very little anxiety about the blizzards you hear of in the N.W. States hurting us. We have them much modified ; only two or three people were frozen to death in Alberta this last one. When it came on we were two and a half miles from home, with Belle and Vi and a slight sleigh. It was awfully sudden, and we could not see ten yards in front of us, and felt nearly suffocated by the wind ; but Belle and Vi knew what was wanted when we turned their heads home, and all we had to do was to hold on while they really tore home straight across the prairie in what, I think, must have been a bee-line for the shack, as we were home in less than no time. Our thermometer did not go below 22° to 17° F. until the wind had subsided, when it went down to -30° F.

We had rather a nice time in the bush, as we were really warm, there being no wind among the trees. We worked all day in our shirt-sleeves. There were only three cold nights, in one of which the thermometer went down to -25° F.—that was our last night there. Three days before, we caught an awfully pretty little brown owl, about four inches long, and his head larger than all the rest of his body ; he was splendid at keeping the mice out of the tent. He was frozen to death on that last night, which was a great pity, as he was very tame, and would eat from the hand. There were no animals to be seen, except birds, though we saw lots of wolf-trail, and heard them howling and yelling all round at night. They woke us up one night when they were killing a cow about a quarter of a mile off; the noise they made then was tremendous. We saw one bear (black) trail, and followed for two miles with our guns, but it got so dark we had to give it up. Next day the trail was covered with snow. By the way, the wolves in the bush are called 'timber jacks,' and are larger and fiercer than the coyote or prairie wolves ; they all have splendid furs on now. I wish I could get some.

During the last week in the bush snow-storms prevented any supplies reaching us, and for the last three days we had beef 'straight,'* with a little baking-powder and treacle to eat with it ; and the beef would

* Beef 'straight' means beef 'and nothing else.'

not have held out for more than two more meals. You say in your last letter that G—— recommends hiding from a blizzard in the snow. As far as I have seen in this country, one could only follow the ostrich's example, and hide one's head and leave the rest to luck —not much use in a blizzard, I think. I said we might be getting some more bronchos any time, as now is the best time to break them. We saw three yesterday, and have arranged to get them if the owner will sell at our price—$240 (£48) for the three.

February.—The day before yesterday I rode over to S—— Creek. I was to join another fellow there, and together we were going to ride up the creek and ' spy out the land.' He never turned up, so I slept at a ' shack ' there, and came back next morning. I saw one section of land which I thought would have suited us; but it was not possible to examine it properly, as the weather was so

bad.   I suppose you have heard by this time
that we have bought three new mares—wild
bronchos.   They are getting quite gentle
now, though two of them are still very
nervous, one three-year old especially.   The
other day we hitched one into the waggon
with Vi.   She ran quite a bit, and Dick
says that he had, for about ten minutes, the
roughest ride he has ever experienced.   We
also got a little cayeuse, or Indian pony, to do
our rough riding, till the others are better
able to stand it.   It was on him that I rode
over to S—— Creek.   When I started I
left Dick laughing at me.   He said I was
quite as big as the pony, and ought to take
my turn at carrying.

We are having glorious weather now.
The snow is nearly all gone.   It freezes
about 20° at night, but thaws during the
day; in fact, the winter seems to have quite
broken up.   Last night, however, there was
a snowstorm, and the temperature stood at

2°. The roads, as you may imagine, are in a pretty bad condition. In driving to Calgary to-day, I came across a cutting where there was about six feet of water and slush. Consequently I had to go down a place which was something very like perpendicular. I give a small plan of the incline, which is no exaggeration at all.

Belle and Vi had to stiffen all four legs and slide for about twelve feet, to get down without upsetting. I had to brace my feet against the front of the box, and lean back with all my might, holding on to the reins, in order to keep them up. Happily the snow was pretty deep, so it was not so slippery as it might have been.

March.—We should have written last week, but we were both so awfully busy that we had not time, and I did not feel up to writing last night to catch this morning's mail, as I had just come in from a forty-mile ride, and was a bit tired. We have taken up land here, about twenty-two miles from Calgary, and in a fairly well settled district. We have each homesteaded 160 acres, and each pre-empted 160 acres, making in all 640 acres. It is a nice little valley, well sheltered on all sides, and with lots of natural hay on it, and within easy reach of timber ; it is about a quarter of a mile from Sheep Creek, a good-sized stream, which boasts of splendid trout fishing. We shall also buy eighty acres of Canadian Pacific Railway land that is adjoining it, in order to get possession of certain springs, which are open all the year round. We shall be allowed ten years to pay for it, so it will be all right, not more than £8 a year. It is almost necessary to buy this eighty acres, if not absolutely, as the land we have taken ʿup would decrease in value if we did not, as there is not water on it through the winter. If we did not take this section, we should have to go much further off, or take up an inferior one.

Belle had her first long ride yesterday (about forty miles), and came through the ordeal very well indeed, though she was a bit tired. In the evening I went to her and found her lying down; I sat on her shoulder and patted her. She was not a bit frightened; most horses won't stand anyone near them when they are lying down. We bought a stallion last Saturday for $225 (£45); it was a very good bargain, and a chance not often got, or we should not have bought it. It took down our cash account quite a bit; but as we shall be working out all the summer, it will be no inconvenience, and we have no debts. It will save us its own value in two years, besides the work it does; and it is a splendid team horse, and wonderfully gentle. We shall camp out in a tent on our land next week, I think, and put up a log-house, and do a little fencing and ploughing. Then we shall work out till the winter, except for three weeks to put up our own hay. Herbert is at C—— Ranche, about eighteen miles west of Calgary, buying another mare. We shall sell our saddle-pony and one of our saddles to help pay for her. You thought in your last letter that going in for horses would bring us into connection with a low set. But here it is quite different; two-thirds of the ranchers go in for cattle, and it is impossible to draw a distinction between cattle-dealers and horse-dealers regarding their characters; from what I have seen, the proportion of gentlemen among horse-raisers is quite as great as among cattlemen and farmers. Our experience of them is that they are very decent fellows, and quite straight, and bearing excellent characters through the country. In fact, the horse-dealers are quite a different sort of people here to some that are to be found in England, though there are black sheep here as well as anywhere else. We were at an auction the other day, and bought a mower, rake, and stove, and two or three other things, very cheap, which saved us quite a bit ; among other things we picked up a turning-lathe, very cheap ; it will come in handy in winter evenings. Our money is invested as safely as it could be ; and as we mean to do a lot of work this summer, we hope to show you a model ranche when you come to see us.

We send you the temperature (Fahrenheit) for January, to give you an idea of our worst month.

		A.M.	A.M.	P.M.
January	1st	1...-16°	10...26°	10... -3°
„	2nd	8... 15°		10... 3°
„	3rd	10... 9°		10... -9°
„	4th	11...-10°	Lowest at night -18°	
„	5th	8...-17°	„	-25°
„	6th	9...-20°	„	-8°
„	7th	9... -6°	„	-16°

		A.M.		P.M.
January	8th	9... -8°	Lowest at night	-10°
„	9th	7... 12°	„	24°
„	10th	10... 0°	„	-4°
„	11th	10... 28°	„	24°
„	12th			
„	13th		Gale of wind.	
„	14th		Thermometer out of order.	
„	15th			
„	16th	10... 0°		
„	17th	10...-11°		
„	18th	10...-20°	Lowest at night	-25°
„	19th	10...-22°	„	-29°
„	20th	8...-25°	„	-12°
„	21st	8...-12°	„	-26°
„	22nd	———		——
„	23rd	8...-20°	„	-26°
„	24th	8... 18°	„	-15°
„	25th	8... 0°	„	-12°
„	26th	8... 22°	„	18°
„	27th	8... 33°	„	18°
„	28th	8... 34°	„	18°
„	29th	8... 34°	„	18°
„	30th	8... 34°	„	18°
„	31st	8... 34°	„	18°

Chinook blowing

S—— Creek.

April.—You will see by the heading of my letter that we have changed camps. We are now living with a fellow whose land adjoins our own, and are working tremendously hard, hauling logs to build our house, and rails to fence with. The house, of course, will take some time. After we have done that, we shall turn to the fencing. We shall want about a mile and a half of that. As soon as the frost goes we shall break thirty acres, as we want to get a crop next spring. We shall have a few potatoes and vegetables in this spring.

A man who lives near here told me the other day that once when he was fishing in the creek he pulled out about eighty pounds of trout. This may be a little tall, but still it shows that the stream is a pretty good one. He said also that none of the fish weighed under a pound.

Last Sunday I had a small adventure with a horse in the pasture here. I was trying to catch him. Well, I got the lasso round his neck, but he got a start on me, and as the ground was very slippery, and I was on foot, I could not stop him, so he pulled me over. I thought that if I hung on to the rope a bit

perhaps he would stop ; but I guess he didn't.
The further he went the faster he went, and
after doing ten miles an hour over hard, rough
frozen ground for the distance of some two
hundred yards, I decided to let go. I got
rather bumped, and am stiff now from it.
Dick then went to the stable to saddle
'Bull' the stallion, and run the horse in.
He had broken out of the pasture, and when
he arrived at the stable, a quarter of a mile
from the hut, there was our friend standing
with Belle and Vi.

You talk about the difficulty of getting
a good house in England now. Here we
have to be thankful if we can't crawl in and
out through the walls. In our last residence
we could see through them on all sides.
However, we have determined that ours shall
be a model house ; I hope the determination
will last.

May.—We have been hard at it all this

month hauling logs and lumber for the house. Three or four days ago we had just started home with a load from the bush where we had been at work, when we got into a morass. The wheels of the waggon sank in as far as the axles. I had just time to get one of the horses on to firm ground ; but Belle sank till she looked as if she were lying on the ground. We unharnessed her, got her out, and started again, having thrown off half the load. We hadn't gone half a dozen yards when she got in again deeper than ever. She pulled till she was so embedded that she could only move her head. We were pretty near two hours before we managed to get her out. She did exactly what we told her in the way of lying still and jumping, or rather trying to jump. At one time I thought we should have had to pull her out with the logging chain and the other horse. We did not get home that night, and had to put up at a friend's house ten miles off.

When there is not a heavy load on the waggons, we ride on the coupling between front and hind wheels. Of course, when we cross S—— Creek, the water comes over this ; and as there is no higher place to go to, we have to grin and bear it.   The water is snow water from the mountains, and, as you'll guess, not remarkable for its warmth. Yesterday we went to Calgary.   When about seventeen miles off we saw a rainstorm coming down from the mountains, so we raced it.   Belle and Vi did the distance without a stop, and hardly seemed at all tired. We arrived ten minutes before the storm.

We got back from Calgary to-day all safe, in spite of mud-holes and swollen creeks. But we nearly all came to grief at F—— Creek, owing to false information.   Two men whom we met told us that it was not too deep to cross with a load.   When we got to the bank it looked to me too deep ; but as they had just crossed, we determined to go by what they said. We hadn't gone three yards when I saw what was up. Still, it was no use turning back then. A few yards more and the horses were out of their depth, and the stream began to take horses, waggon and all along with it. Belle and Vi, however, did not see the fun of this, and did their best to struggle across. Fortunately they got foothold on some shingle. We then waited till the stream slewed the waggon round on to the same bed, and then unhitched them, and got them to the other side. The next business was to unload the waggon as quick as we could, for the water was rising fast. We did all we had time for, and then hitched the two mares on to the end of the waggon-pole. They pulled it out, and about nine hundredweight of lumber with it. Had this happened fifteen feet lower down there would have been little chance of saving either waggon or horses, as the banks are four or five feet high and perpendicular, and there is a good fifteen feet of water. The waggon, too, was pretty heavy, having got thirty-three hundred-weight on board.

By the way, you asked for a description of Dick. He is a little taller than when we came out, and very much broader. His face is the colour of a mahogany sideboard. L—— and I think if he were to appear in B—— in his usual costume, there would be a general stampede out of the town.

P.S.—Mab has got a little colt, which does nothing else but run races all day with its own shadow.

CHAPTER XV.

May.—Having finished chinking and plastering, we are at last installed in our new house, and are very comfortable. It is twenty-four feet by twenty inside, which is considered big in this country ; and, indeed, it seems so to us, after having lived for some time in a house twelve by fourteen. There is a sod roof on, and we are going to put lumber over it, though as yet the rain has not come through. There are two windows, and we shall make another as soon as we have time. Our cellar is six feet square. There is a timber partition up the middle of the house ; in one half we have the stove and cook, in the other we sleep,

14—2

sit, read, etc. There is going to be a veranda in front when we have time.

We have ploughed a fire-break round the place, and a corral to one side of it, to keep the colts in while we are breaking-in their mothers. There is also a ' snubbing-post ' close to the house—that is, a post fixed into the ground very tight, used for tying wild horses to while putting on the saddle or harness during the breaking-in. Our water comes from a hole we dug in the coulée, a few yards in front of the house.

In the room we sleep in there is a table in one corner, a double bed in the one next to it ; in the third corner the big trunk, known generally as the ' Woolwich Infant,' and in the last, a lot of sacks of oats for the horses. We sit, at present, on our two gun-cases placed across two kegs of nails. In the kitchen there is a stove at one end with the cooking things hung up behind it ; a pile of oats heaped up in one corner ; saddles, harness, and bridles in the other.

We have broken-in Queenie to the saddle. When we first put the saddle on her she bucked tremendously, but quieted down afterwards. The next day she bucked even worse than before, and when I got on her, the first thing I knew was that I had lost my stirrups, which were much too long for me, and I slipped on one side, one leg over the saddle and one under her body. It was awfully hard work to hang on while she bucked. I clung with one hand to a strap round the horn of the saddle, and I guess it skinned my knuckles just a bit. Until to-day she used often to run away with us, going round in a circle so small that it seemed possible to touch the centre of it.

We did not buy the Canadian Pacific Railway land after all : they asked too much, and we found water on our own place. There is a clump of timber on one corner of our section, and we can get all we want beyond within a few miles by paying $50 for a 'timber permit.' Timber-land costs $5 an acre, besides the surveying fees. Our house faces south-west, and we get a glorious view of the Rockies, which we can see through the window when lying in bed.

We are trying now to get a contract for putting up hay for some of the people round here. I think we shall manage it.

June.—We are just finishing railing-in our pasture-land. For the last week Dick has stayed all day in the bush cutting and piling rails, while I hauled them down to our place. We landed four loads a day—that is, about 200 rails—and took about two hours and a half to each load ; so you can guess that we have had good busy days. Towards the end of the week Belle and Vi thought that they had had about enough of it, and became rather bad-tempered. They didn't show it to me, but would bite and kick one another.

This summer we intend to break-in a new

team, Mab and Dolly, enlarge our pasture-land to 180 acres, and put up about thirty tons of hay for our own use. Then we want to get a contract for hay at the S—— Creek Ranche. I went to see the manager, and made him an offer ; he will let me know in a day or two whether he takes it or no. I rode over to see him on Queenie. When we got to the river, two dogs began to jump about and bark on the other side ; so my lady insisted on walking down the river till I was just wet through, and madder than anything with her. On the whole, though, she behaves very well, considering that she has only just been broken to the saddle.

Everything round here is looking beautiful just now. The birds are present in flocks. We have had no time for fishing yet, though the river is not 500 yards from us.

Our room looks quite jolly now. We have put up some bookshelves and the photos, also our bats, rackets, and guns. The round

log walls show the things off very well.
Dick has been trying, unsuccessfully, to
sketch the house lately ; but he makes it
look rather like a pigsty, so I won't send
any of his attempts just yet.

July.—We have started putting up our own
hay (twenty-five or thirty tons), and everything is going splendidly. We are having
grand weather ; no rain at all till last night,
when there was a short storm which could do
us no harm, as we had stacked all the hay
that was raked up. We have ten tons in the
stack, and about as much more lying on the
ground cut. To-morrow morning I shall
hope to cut enough to finish it. After that,
I have twenty-five tons to cut and rake for a
neighbour (at 75c. per ton). This will be
three days' work. Then we start on a contract we have got for the R—— Ranche, at
$2.62½ per ton. This we expect will keep
us going to the middle of September. After

that we come back to our own place, and put up stables, and fix up generally for the winter, besides training Queenie for the October races. Since she has been broken in she has shown a good deal of speed, and two or three fellows have been after her. One man offered me a big mare and a horse for her. We hope she will take the half-mile or three-quarters of a mile. We expect to clear over $300 on the 200 tons contract. If we do, we shall be able to put in the whole time till next haying on our own place.

Yesterday, as I was running the mower, driving Vi and Mab, Mab's colt kept getting in the way, and had one or two near shaves of getting her feet cut off in the knives. So I stopped the machine, and we tried to catch her. As we had no long rope to lasso her in the open, we ran her into the corral and roped her there. Though only ten weeks old, she fought furiously. I did not think she was strong enough to do any harm, and so was slightly careless how I handled her. She suddenly got up on her hind-legs, and hit me on the nose with one of her forefeet, making it bleed and knocking me down. After that I was more careful. Mab and Dolly are now broken, and are wonderfully gentle.

A few days ago we went fishing for two evenings, and caught *seventy-four* trout, running from half a pound to two pounds and a half. The whole outfit weighed seventy-seven pounds. Two rods were going one day and one the next. The baits we used were little gilt minnows and salmon-flies, also spoon-bait of the size used for black bass. For about an hour the first evening, they would get on just as fast as you could throw the minnow in, haul the fish in, and unhook him. One big one got away from Dick with a spoon, and another with a minnow, in each case breaking the gimp.

There is an awful quantity of mosquitoes here now. In the early morning or evening, we cannot do any work without a smoke to work by; and we have to set smudges (smokes) going for the horses.

On Friday I came across a piece of ground where one could make a tennis-lawn very easily. It is quite level and very fairly smooth.

Hay Camp.

September.—You will be surprised at not having heard from us before, but I have been quite unable to post a letter, though I've had one written in my pocket for some days. We have been camped here for about a month. We got the contract that I mentioned before, and have got to get the hay up by September 15th. There are 200 tons of it. We had about ten days' wet weather to start with, which delayed us a good deal, so now we have to rustle in good earnest. We have been working seven days in a week, from 5 a.m. to 8 p.m. I think we shall just manage it if the weather holds.

I'm afraid you would not think much of
our camp if you saw it. The cooking place
is just eight feet square, and consists of four
posts in the ground, and a few boards nailed
on to three sides. Our sleeping-place is a
tent eleven feet long by six broad. Four
of us sleep in it ; and it is lucky that the
nights are cool, or we should be roasted
alive.

Last night we helped to tie up a wild cow
a hundred yards from camp. A cow-boy had
separated a cow from the herd, and was trying
to drive it to the ranche to be killed for beef ;
but as he was on a bad horse he could not do
it. He lassoed it over the horns, and yelled
to us to bring a rope and help him. The
end of his lasso was round the horn of his
saddle, and he was holding it in. We went
up just outside the cow's reach to throw a
rope round its forelegs. The cow made for
us, and the lasso became so tight that the
cow's horns touching it now and then made

it sound like a banjo string ; if it had broken there would have been some ticklish work, as the cow was perfectly furious. However, we managed to throw it over, and then it was killed.

September.—At last we are through with our hay contract. It has only got to be measured and paid for now. We were awfully glad when it was finished, and have been taking it easy ever since. We have put up another three tons for ourselves, and I have cut about ten tons more for a neighbour. Most of our time, however, since the 15th, has been employed in shooting and fishing. Some of the fish we catch are being salted for the winter. Dick goes down regularly in the morning and catches about fifteen pounds of trout. Yesterday we both went, and just at the south-west corner of our place we found fresh deer trail, and a few minutes later saw two deer. Unfortunately, we only had shot-guns with us, and loaded with small shot, so we had to leave them. The ducks are now in full swing, and the geese are beginning to show up. Also there are quite a number of prairie chickens around.

We ought to come out of our hay contract pretty well, I think. It has cost us about $150 in labour and provisions, and we ought to get somewhere between $550 and $600 for it.

October.—I have only just time to write a line. We had rather a misfortune last Saturday afternoon. Nearly half our contract hay was burnt by a prairie fire just before the ranche took it over. Thus the loss falls on us. About seventy or eighty tons went, worth $200, so that we shall only clear about $125 now for our summer's work. We had to put in all Saturday night keeping a look-out on the fire, and since we came

home have had a saddle-horse always ready
in case of a wind getting up and scattering
the burning hay over the prairie, and firing
the range. There are two big fires raging
around ; one twenty miles off, the other
about six. They will not trouble us however, unless a big west wind gets up.

I was out shooting this afternoon, and got
four brace—three brace of prairie chicken,
and one brace of ruffled grouse, called wood-
partridges here. There are immense quantities of game round here, but one is entirely
dependent on luck in putting them up without a dog. When T—— comes out he
ought to bring a setter. It would really pay,
as we could then, without any difficulty, keep
the house supplied with fresh meat. While
I was shooting Dick was fishing, and caught
two trout, one weighing two pounds and the
other two and a half pounds. To-morrow
we go into Calgary to get some things for
the winter. After that we shall not, I hope,

have to take a team in till next spring. Bull goes with us to be sold, though I'm afraid it is rather a bad time of year for selling.

THE END.

BILLING AND SONS, PRINTERS, GUILDFORD.

www.ingramcontent.com/pod-product-compliance
Lightning Source LLC
Chambersburg PA
CBHW020106030726
47498CB00006B/1981